THE POISONOUS PLANS OF
PROFESSOR WEIRD

STEVE BARLOW • STEVE SKIDMORE
ILLUSTRATED BY PIPI SPOSITO

Franklin Watts
First published in Great Britain in 2020
by The Watts Publishing Group

Text © Steve Barlow and Steve Skidmore 2020
Illustrations © Franklin Watts 2020
Design: Cathryn Gilbert

The authors and illustrator have asserted their rights in
accordance with the Copyright, Designs and Patents Act, 1988.

ISBN 978 1 4451 7003 9
ebook ISBN 978 1 4451 7004 6
Library ebook ISBN 978 1 4451 7005 3

1 3 5 7 9 10 8 6 4 2

Printed in Great Britain

Franklin Watts
An imprint of
Hachette Children's Group
Part of The Watts Publishing Group
Carmelite House
50 Victoria Embankment
London EC4Y 0DZ

An Hachette UK Company
www.hachette.co.uk

www.franklinwatts.co.uk

HOW TO BE A MEGAHERO

Some superheroes can read books with their X-ray vision without opening the covers or even when they're in a different room ...

Others can read them while flying through the air or stopping a runaway train.

But that stuff *IS* just small potatoes to you, because you're not a superhero. You're a *MEGAHERO*!

YES, this book is about **YOU**! And you don't just read it to the end and then stop. You read a bit: then you make a choice that takes you to a different part of the book. You might jump from Section 3 to 47 or 28!

If you make a good choice, *GREAT!*

BUUUUUUT ...

If you make the wrong choice ... *DA-DA-DAAAH!*

ALL KINDS OF BAD STUFF WILL HAPPEN.

Too bad! It's no good turning green and tearing your shirt off. You'll just have to start again. But that won't happen, will it?

Because you're not a zero, or even a superhero. You are ... *MEGAHERO*!

You are a **BRILLIANT INVENTOR** — but one day **THE SUPER PARTICLE-ACCELERATING COSMIC RAY COLLIDER** you'd made out of old drinks cans, lawnmower parts and a mini black hole went critical and scrambled your molecules (nasty!). When you finally stopped screaming, smoking and bouncing off the walls, you found your body had changed! Now you can transform into any person, creature or object. HOW AWESOME IS THAT?!!!

You communicate with your **MEGACOMPUTER** companion, **PAL**, through your **MEGASHADES** sunglasses (which make you look pretty COOL, too). **PAL** controls the things you turn into and *almost hardly ever crashes and has to be turned off and on again!* This works perfectly — unless you have a bad WIFI signal, or **PAL** gets something wrong — but hey! That's computers for you, right?

Like all heroes, your job is to SAVE THE WORLD from **BADDIES AND THEIR EVIL SCHEMES**. But be back in time for supper. Even **MEGAHEROES** have to eat ...

Go to 1.

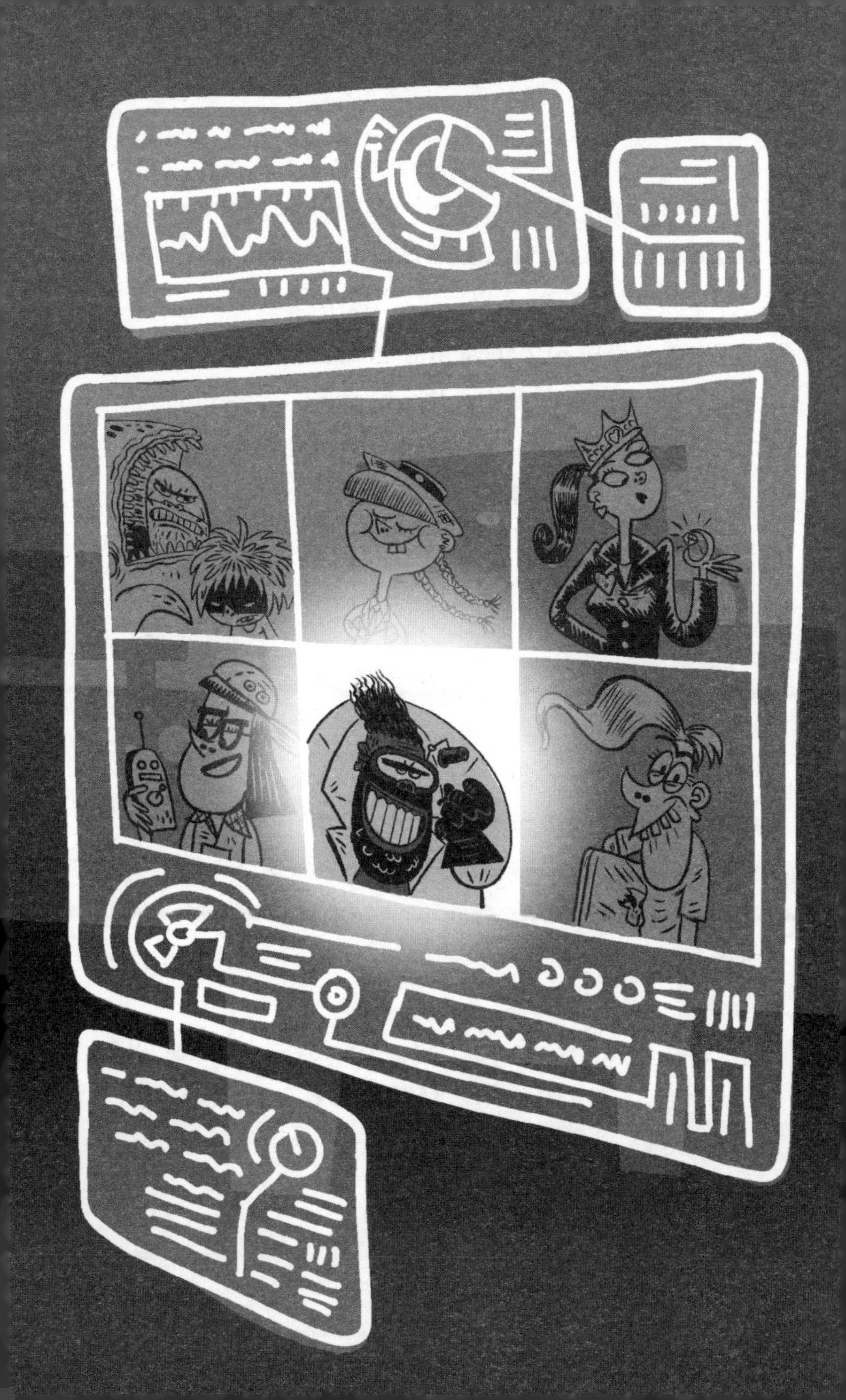

1

You are in the ***MEGA*** cave inventing some new ***MEGA*** gadgets when the ***MEGA*** alarm sounds ...

"INCOMING **MEGA** MESSAGE," says PAL.

"The world probably needs saving again," you sigh. "Who is it?"

"THE CITY MAYOR ..."

"Put her on ..."

The screen lights up to reveal a very hairy figure!

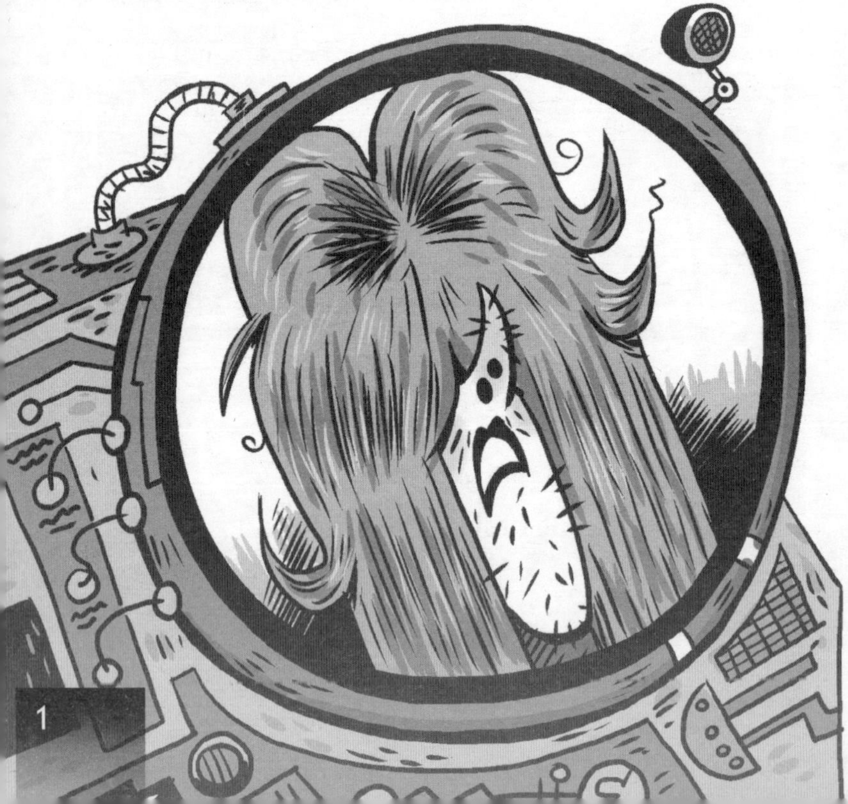

Hmmm, you think, *that's strange!* You put on your ***MEGA*** good manners voice. "If you don't mind me saying, Mayor, you seem to be a little bit more hairy than last time we spoke."

"Yes," replies the mayor. "I have a ***MEGA*** hair problem. I need your help."

If you wish to listen to the mayor, go to 18.

If you want to tell her to see a hairdresser, not a *MEGAHERO*, go to 33.

2

You head back into the main factory. After searching around you see a door with a sign.

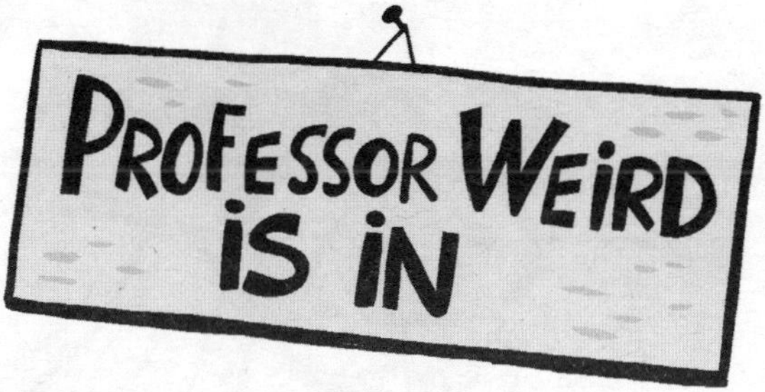
PROFESSOR WEIRD
IS IN

To head inside, go to 32.

To check it out first using your shades, go to 9.

3

With no leads to follow, you head back to the ***MEGA*** cave where PAL has some bad news.

"THE MAYOR HAS BEEN BACK IN TOUCH. SHE'S NOT HAPPY WITH THE TIME IT'S TAKING. SHE'S GOT ANOTHER HERO TO DEAL WITH IT. SHE'S CALLED IN **THE MARVELLOUS MONKEY** AND THROWING YOU OFF THE CASE."

How embarrassing. You've been replaced by a MONKEY! *Go back to 1.*

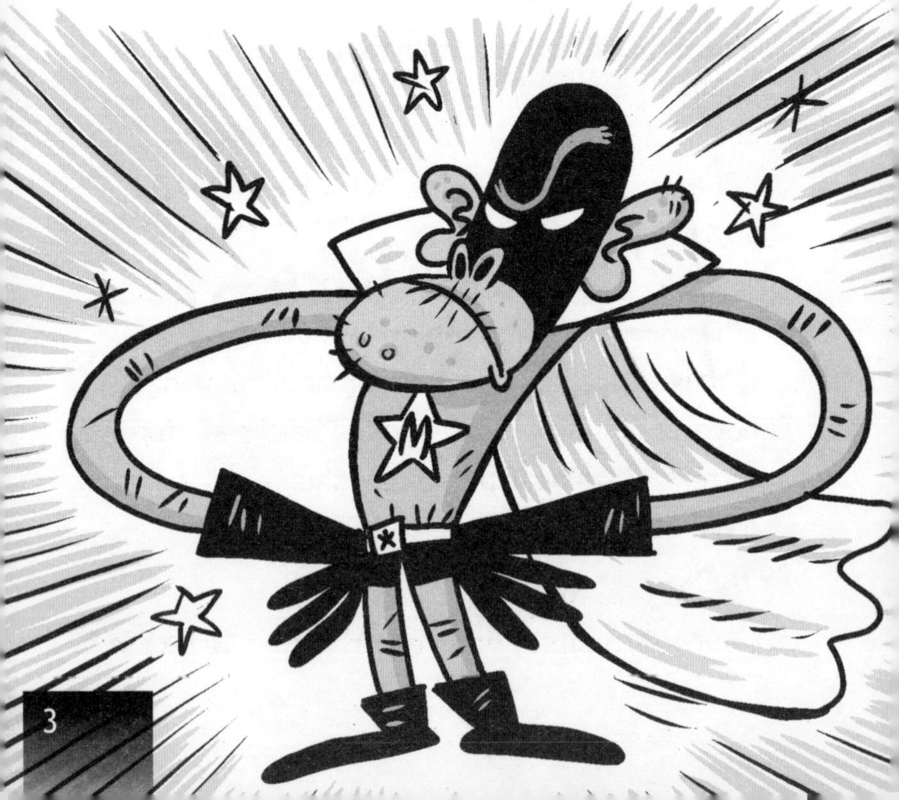

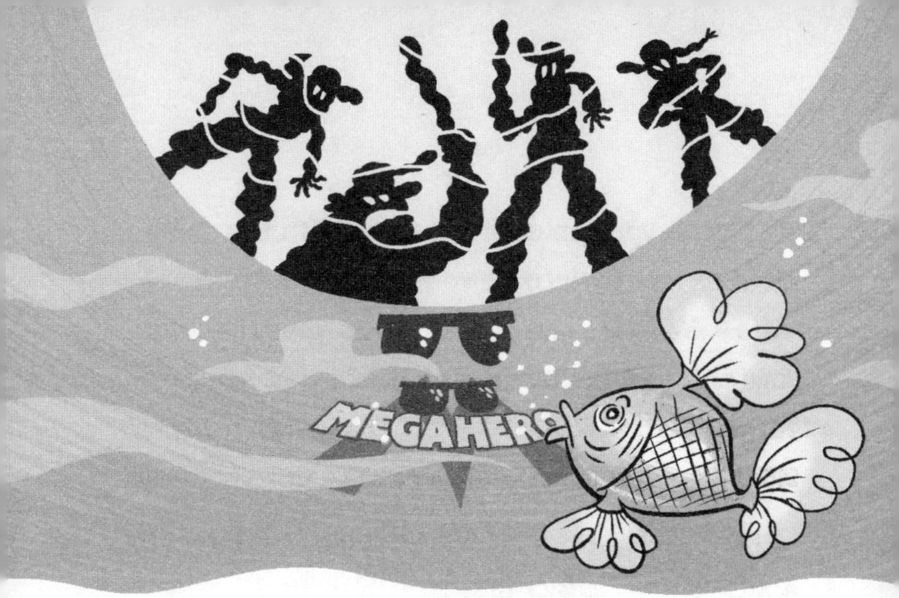
MEGAHERO

4

"Turn me into a tank," you tell **PAL**.

Seconds later you are frozen still and feeling soaked with a goldfish swimming around your insides!

"I meant an **ARMY TANK**, not a **FISH TANK**," you say.

"WELL, BE MORE SPECIFIC!" replies PAL.

"Don't move!" commands a booming voice.

You look up to see several guards standing above you holding large wooden batons. Before you can react, you hear the leader shout, "Smash it!"

The goldfish gulps!

DA-DA-DAAAH!

Bubble, bubble, you're in trouble! ***Go back to 1.***

5

As a falcon you can easily keep up with the cloud.

But as you fly into it, you realise you've made a ***MEGA MISTAKE***. The cloud fills up your tiny bird lungs and hair begins to sprout between your feathers!

You try to communicate with PAL but your beak is full of hair!

"***PAARGGGHHH***," you splutter.

The growing hair weighs you down, causing you to plummet helplessly towards a very hard concrete road.

DA-DA-DAAAH!

PAL couldn't "HAIR" your squawks!

Go back to 1.

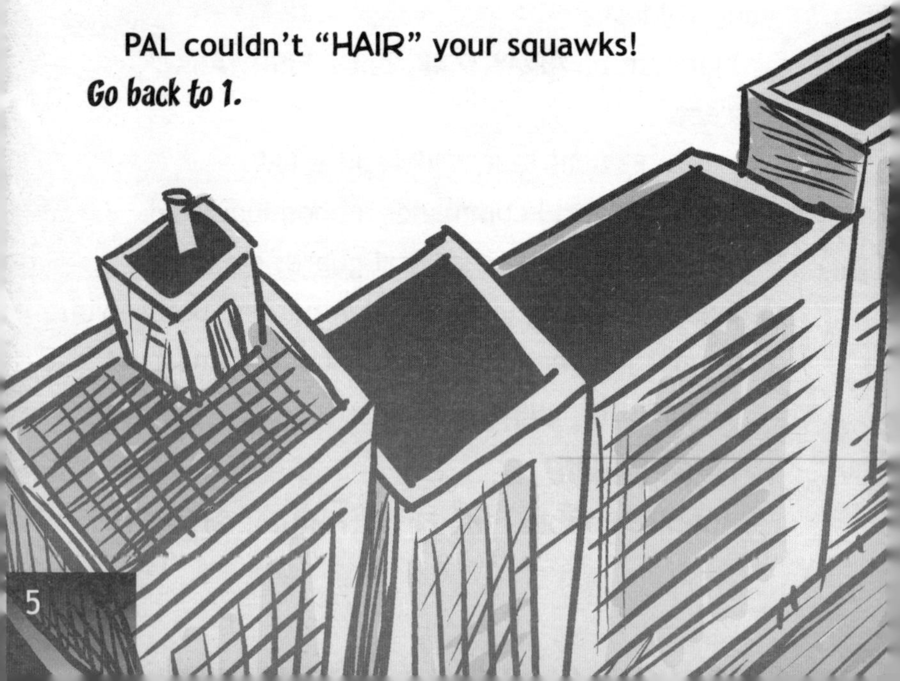

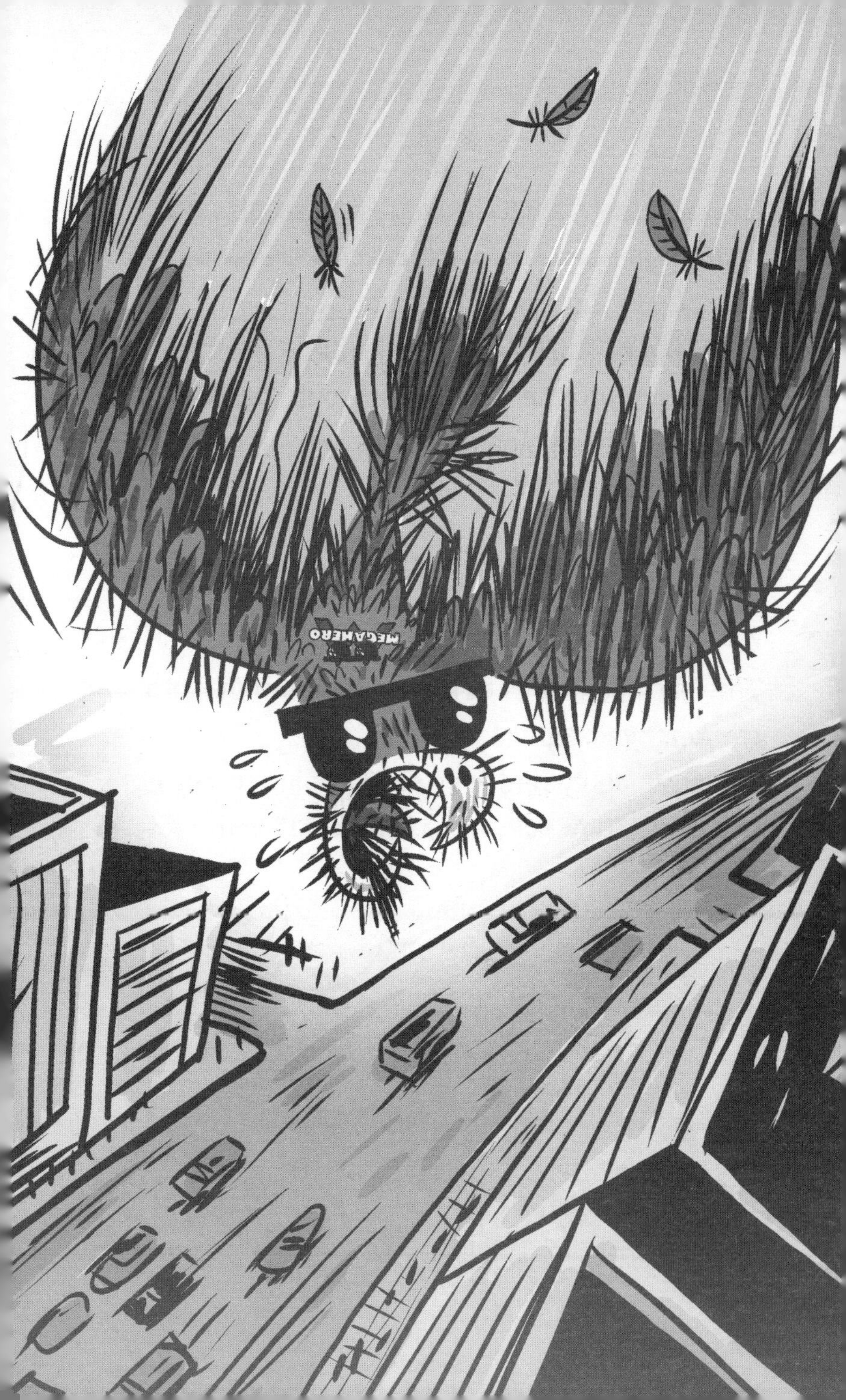
MEGAMERO

6

"Get ready for anything weird and sneaky, PAL," you whisper and turn back into human form. "I accept your surrender, Professor."

"**MWAHHAHAHAHAHA!**" he laughs. "You think I'm telling you the truth! That would be **WEIRD!** Of course I have plenty of gas in the tank! Prepare for **HAIR!**"

Go to 34.

7

The machine begins to move off. "Turn me into a tracker," you tell PAL.

You suddenly find yourself dropping through the air. "A **TRACKER**, not a **CRACKER**!" you scream.

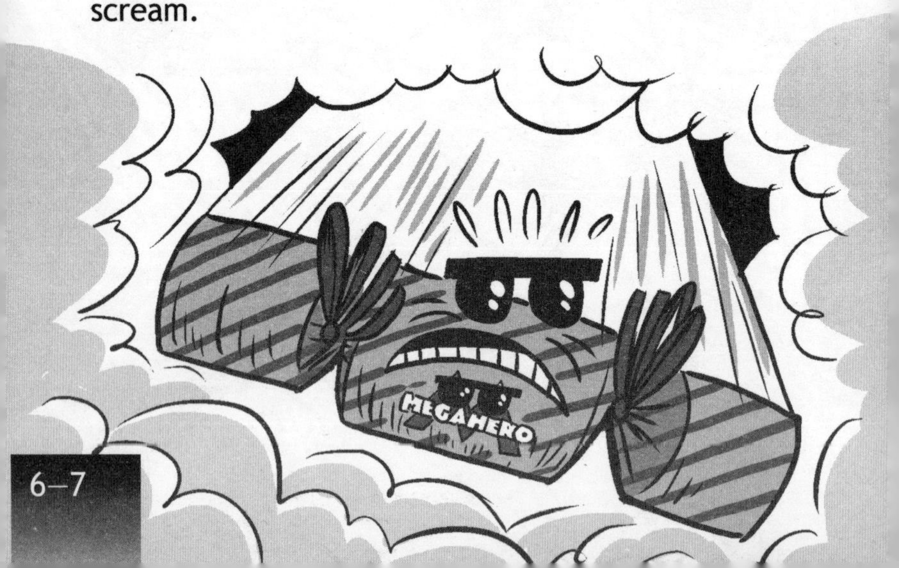
MEGAHERO

"**OOOPS**, SORRY!"

You change into a drone with a radar GPS tracking system.

"LUCKILY YOU **PULLED** THROUGH," says PAL. "**PULL – CRACKER**. IT'S A JOKE," says PAL.

"Not in this universe," you snap back.

Go to 48.

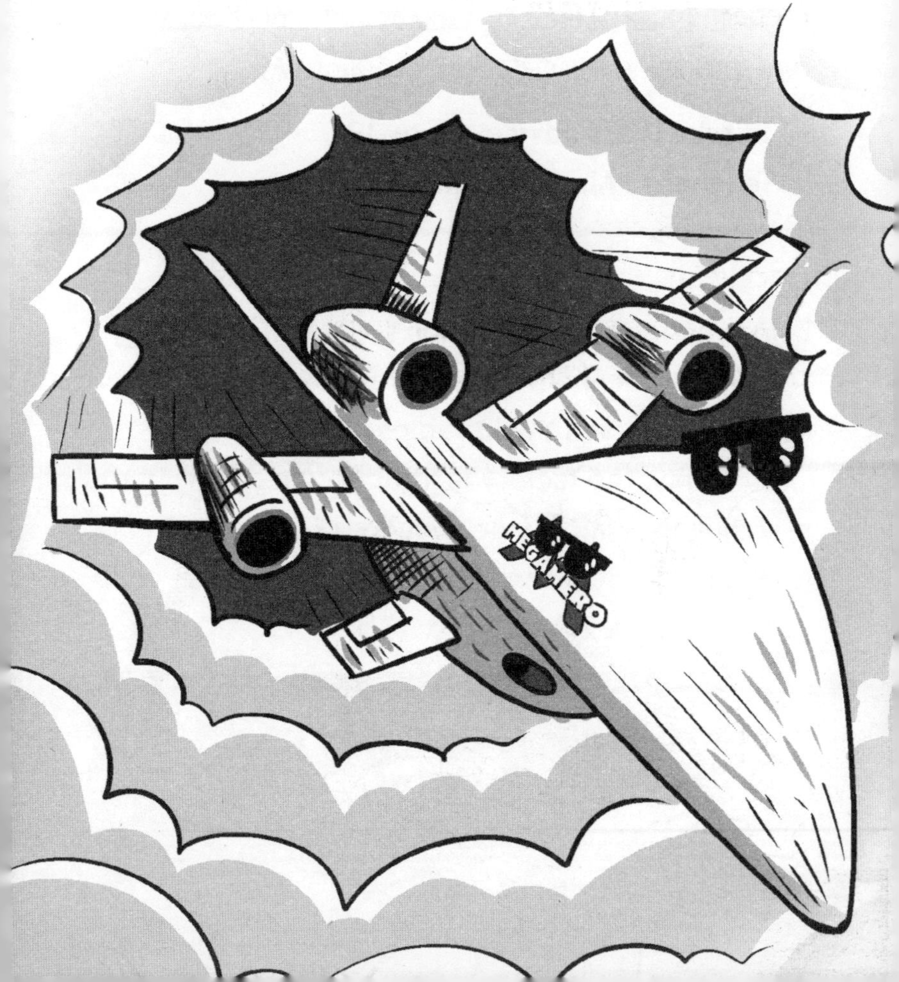
MEGAMERO

8

"I need to see this cloud for myself," you tell
PAL. "I'll head downtown straight away. What
do you suggest I should turn into?"

"SOMETHING THAT IS NON-LIVING," replies PAL.

"I'm not turning into a vampire," you reply.
"That would be ridiculous!"

"I DIDN'T MEAN UNDEAD, I MEANT YOU SHOULD TURN
INTO SOMETHING NON-ORGANIC!" explains PAL.

To take PAL's advice, go to 39.
To ignore PAL, go to 14.

9

Using your **MEGA X-RAY** vision specs, you look
through the door. There is nothing inside the
room. *A trap,* you think. *I'm not going in.*

Suddenly, the factory is lit up by dozens of
searchlights. Half-blinded you look up and see
a familiar figure sitting in a flying car!

"Hello, Professor Weird!"

"Hello, Megahero. Or rather, **MEDDLING** Hero!"

To speak to the professor, go to 37.
To attack him, go to 15.

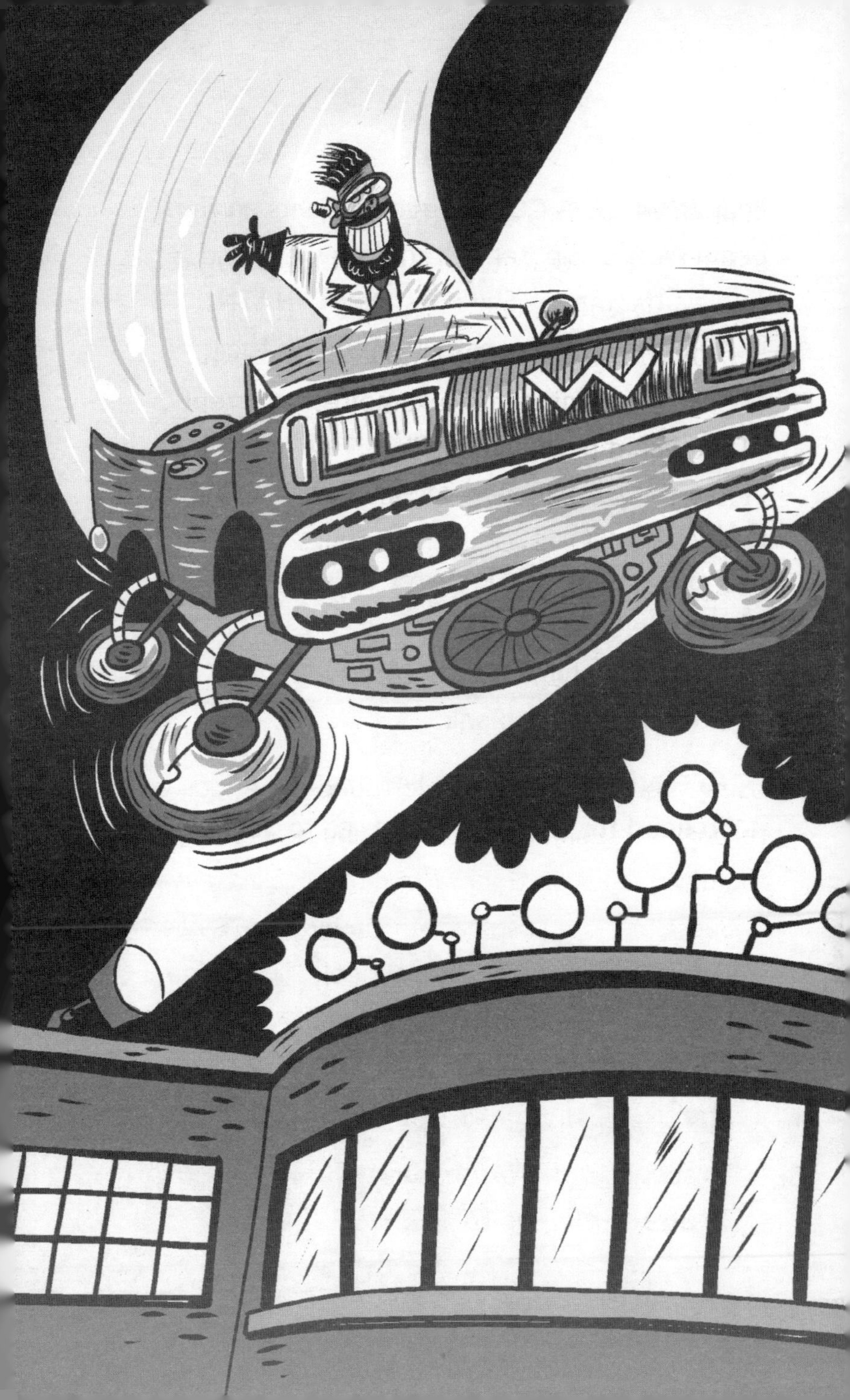

10

Your ***MEGA*** specs **COMMS** screen lights up to beam PAL's computer system into view, and reveals the mayor. She now has **NO HAIR**!

"Did the hairdresser overdo it with the scissors?"

"No!" she snaps. "Another cloud has just appeared. It's pink and is making everybody **BALD**! It's weird!"

"You're right! It's Professor Weird behind this. I'm on the case!"

"Then stop him, Megahero!"

The screen goes blank.

To search for Professor Weird, go to 27.

To head for the pink cloud, go to 38.

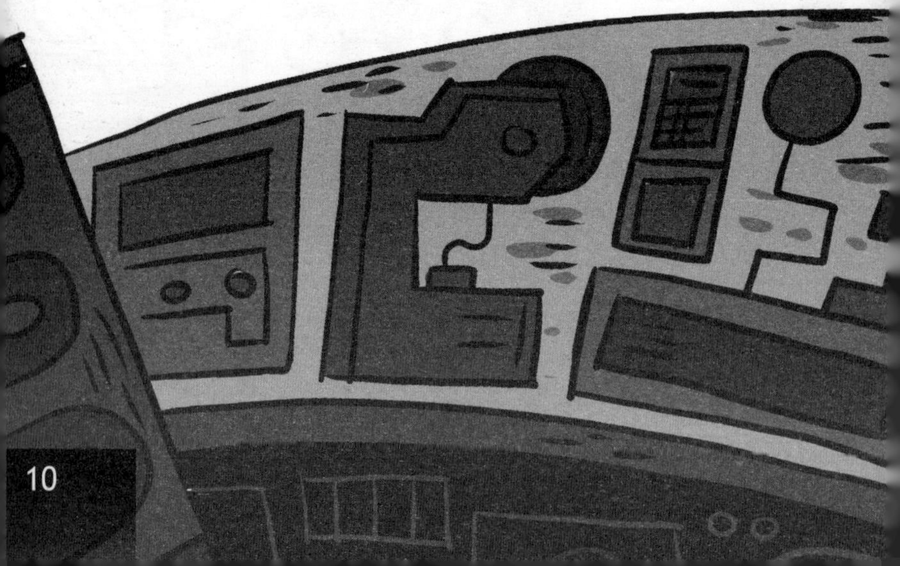

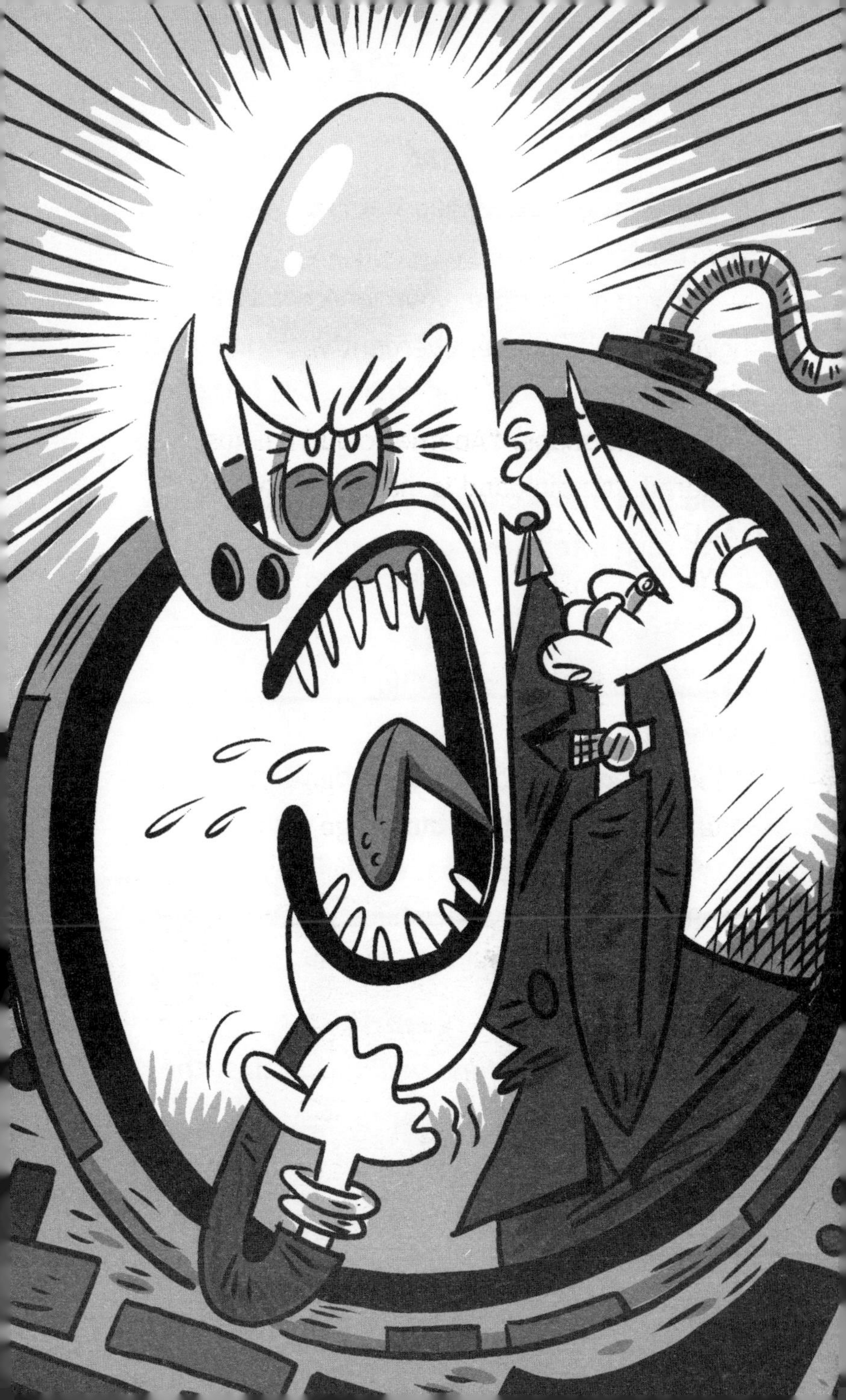

11

"I'll stay as a drone," you tell PAL. "I think it will ..."

But you don't finish your sentence as a lightning bolt shoots out from the cloud and hits you full on! Your electric circuits are frazzled and you plunge earthwards.

To turn into a parachute, go to 29.
To turn into a helicopter, go to 44.

12

"PAL, turn me into something small," you whisper.

You change into a beetle and scurry away to hide under a chemical tank.

"You can't escape that easily," says the professor. "I know you're here, somewhere." He shoots a gas cloud towards the tanks.

To try and escape, go to 19.
To stand and defend yourself against the cloud, go to 45.

13

A huge neon sign sits on top of the factory.

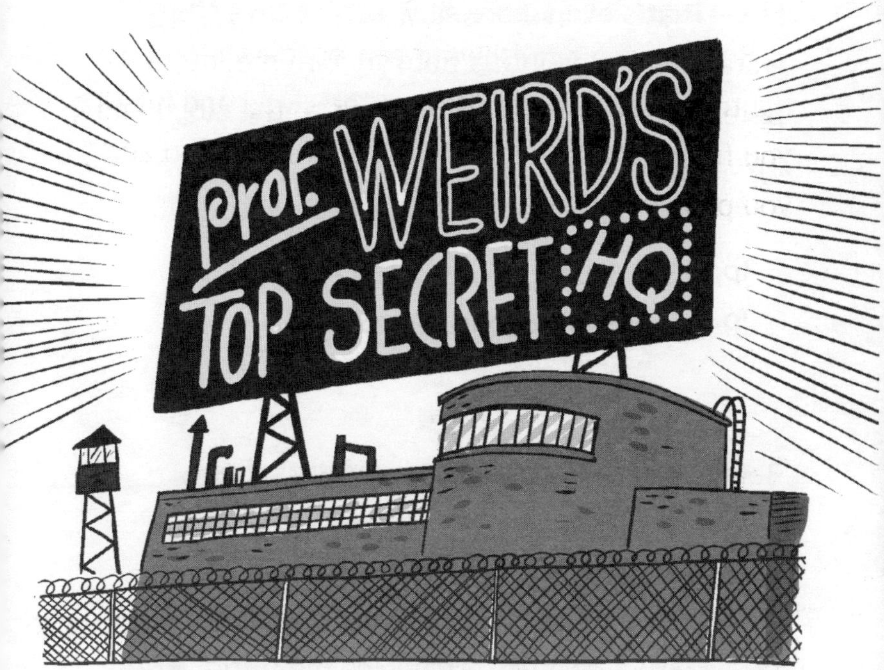
Prof. WEIRD'S
TOP SECRET HQ

Not that top secret, you think. *How weird!*

The factory is surrounded by watchtowers and razor wire fences. Armed guards patrol the grounds.

To dig your way in, go to 30.
To blast your way in, go to 4.
To sneak your way in, go to 24.

14

"What, like a non-organic vegetable?" you say. "That's even more silly. I can't save the world by turning into a potato! Turn me into a peregrine falcon and I can speed to the cloud and investigate it closely."

"I DON'T THINK THAT'S A GOOD IDEA," warns PAL.

To listen to PAL, go to 39.
To turn into a falcon, go to 49.

15

Before you can attack, the professor shoots a cloud of gas at you. You cough and splutter before the gas quickly disperses.

"Ha, you'll have to do better than that, Professor," you laugh. "PAL turn me into a *MEGA* weapon."

Nothing happens.

"PAL, I'm waiting!" you say.

"I'M TRYING," replies PAL. "YOUR **MEGA** SYSTEM ISN'T RESPONDING!"

Go to 40.

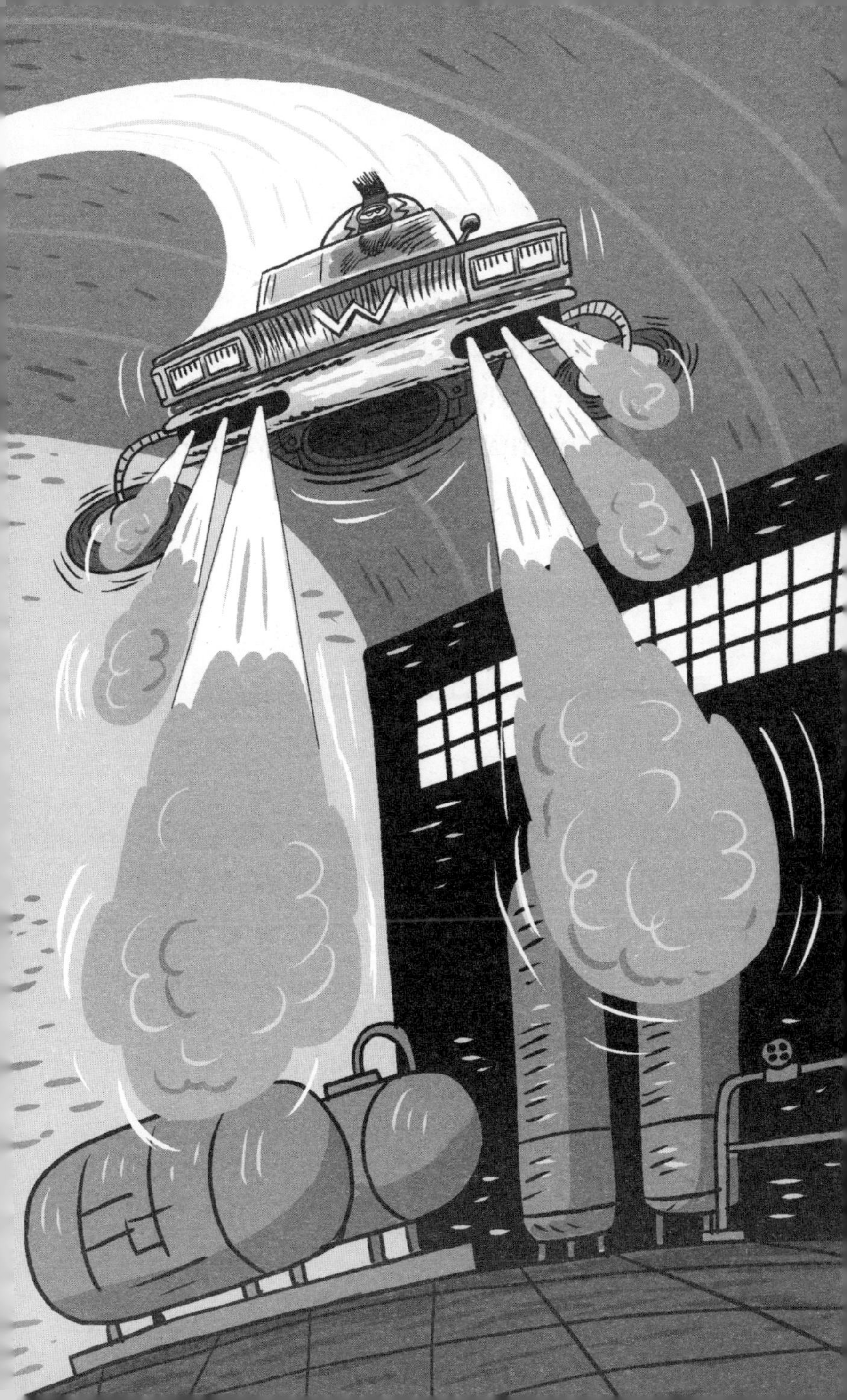

16

"Any news on who might be behind this?" you ask PAL.

"ALL MY CALCULATIONS LEAD ME TO BELIEVE THERE'S ONLY ONE PERSON WHO IS WEIRD ENOUGH TO CARRY OUT SUCH A HAIR-BRAINED SCHEME," replies PAL.

"I think I can guess," you reply. "My old *MEGA* enemy, PROFESSOR WEIRD!"

"CORRECT!"

To get more information on Professor Weird, go to 31.

To hunt him down IMMEDIATELY, go to 47.

17

You sneak into the drone hangar. There are hundreds of machines identical to the one you've already seen.

What in MEGA name is the professor planning? you wonder.

At that moment the drones light up. The roof slides open and the machines rise into the air!

To destroy the drones, go to 28.

To close the roof, go to 43.

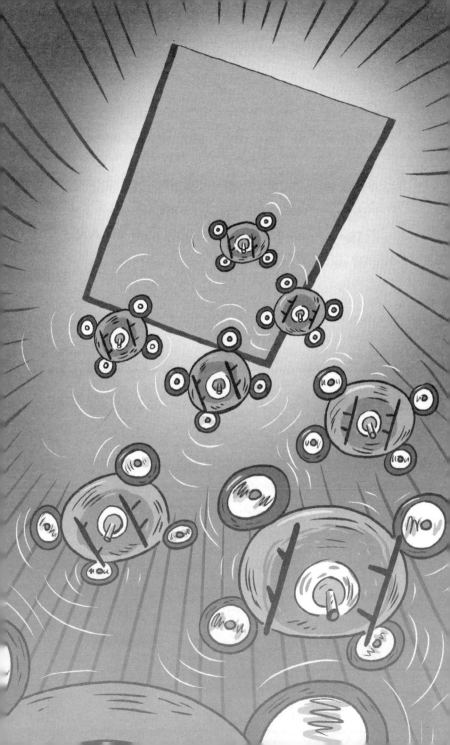

"What is this hairy problem?" you ask the mayor.

"This morning a strange green cloud appeared covering the city streets."

"Just sounds like bad pollution," you say.

"It's not!" says the mayor. "Anyone who was outside suddenly started growing hair. I stepped out of my car, breathed in and now look at me. Even the animals of the city have been affected!

Nobody wants to come out of their homes or offices. The city is at a standstill."

"What do you want me to do?" you ask.

"I think someone is behind this. I need you to find out who it is and why they are doing it. And now I've got to go to the hairdresser's!"

To investigate the green cloud immediately, go to 8.

To get PAL to run a check on possible suspects, go to 46.

19

You turn back into human form and sprint for the exit, but you are too slow. The cloud covers you. Coughing and spluttering you contact PAL.

"Turn me into a fan, so I can blow this cloud away."

Nothing happens.

Go to 40.

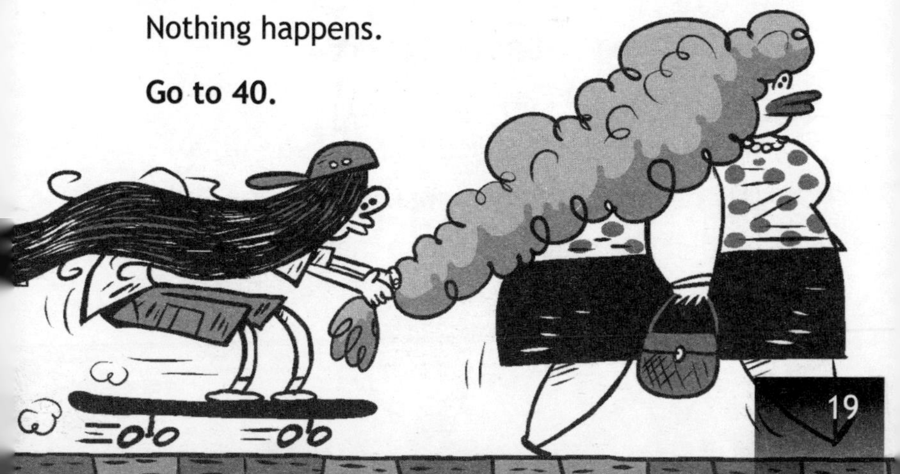

20

You shoot into the middle of the pink cloud but quickly realise that you've made a **MEGA** mistake. The concentrated chemical cloud reacts with the rocket's metal causing it to blister and melt! You try to contact PAL but it is too late. You're dissolving!

DA-DA-DAAAH!

What a drip! Go back to 1.

21

You realise that you need to stay in a non-organic state to avoid becoming hairy very quickly.

"PAL, turn me into a drone," you order.

You become a long, narrow white thing with knobbly ends that seems to have dropped off a pirate flag.

"Not a **BONE**, a **DRONE**!" you cry.

"SORRY!"

In seconds you find yourself turned into a highly-decorated golden chair standing in the middle of the road, unable to move.

"I said a **DRONE** not a **THRONE**!" you shout.

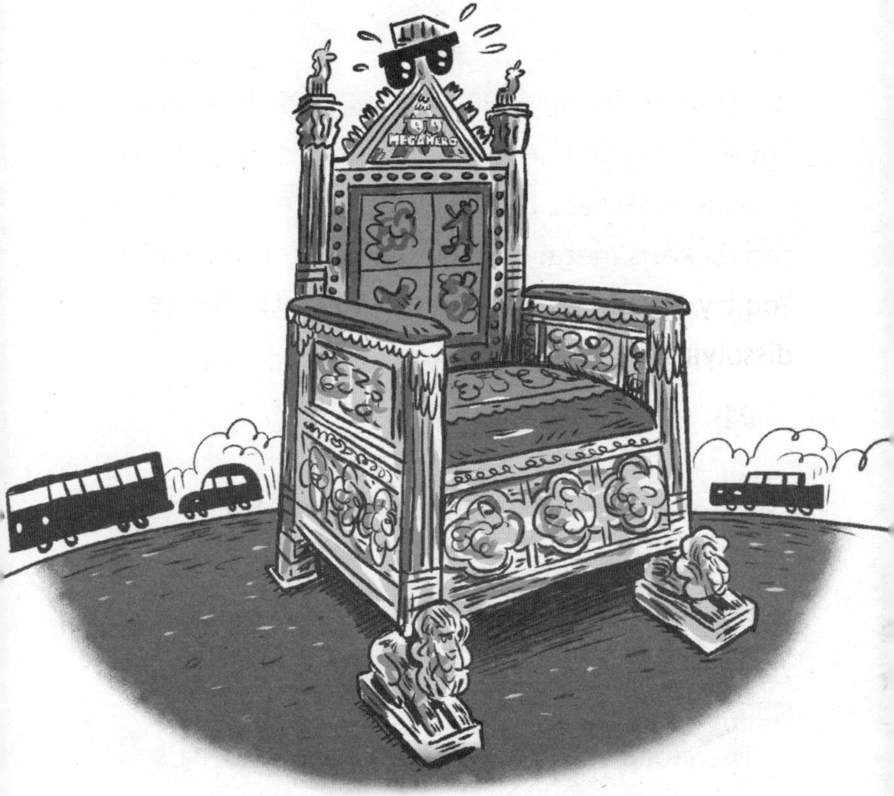
MEGAHERO

"**OOOPS** – MY BAD, OR RATHER MY BAD SIGNAL," replies PAL. The computer rectifies the mistake and turns you into a drone. Seconds later you are shooting skywards and chasing down the cloud.

To see where the cloud is heading, go to 36.

To fly into the cloud and analyse it, go to 42.

22

You head to the lab door and turn the handle. The door opens.

That's strange, you wonder, *why isn't a* **TOP SECRET LAB** *locked?*

To head inside, go to 32.

To check out the drone hangar, go to 17.

23

"We need to destroy that cloud," you tell PAL. "Any ideas?"

PAL turns you into a Chinook helicopter.

"Sweet move!" you say and set your rotors spinning.

The cloud immediately breaks up, leaving a strange-looking flying machine with a huge nozzle blower.

So that's how the cloud was made and why it could move, you think.

To destroy the cloud-making machine, go to 35.

To track it, go to 7.

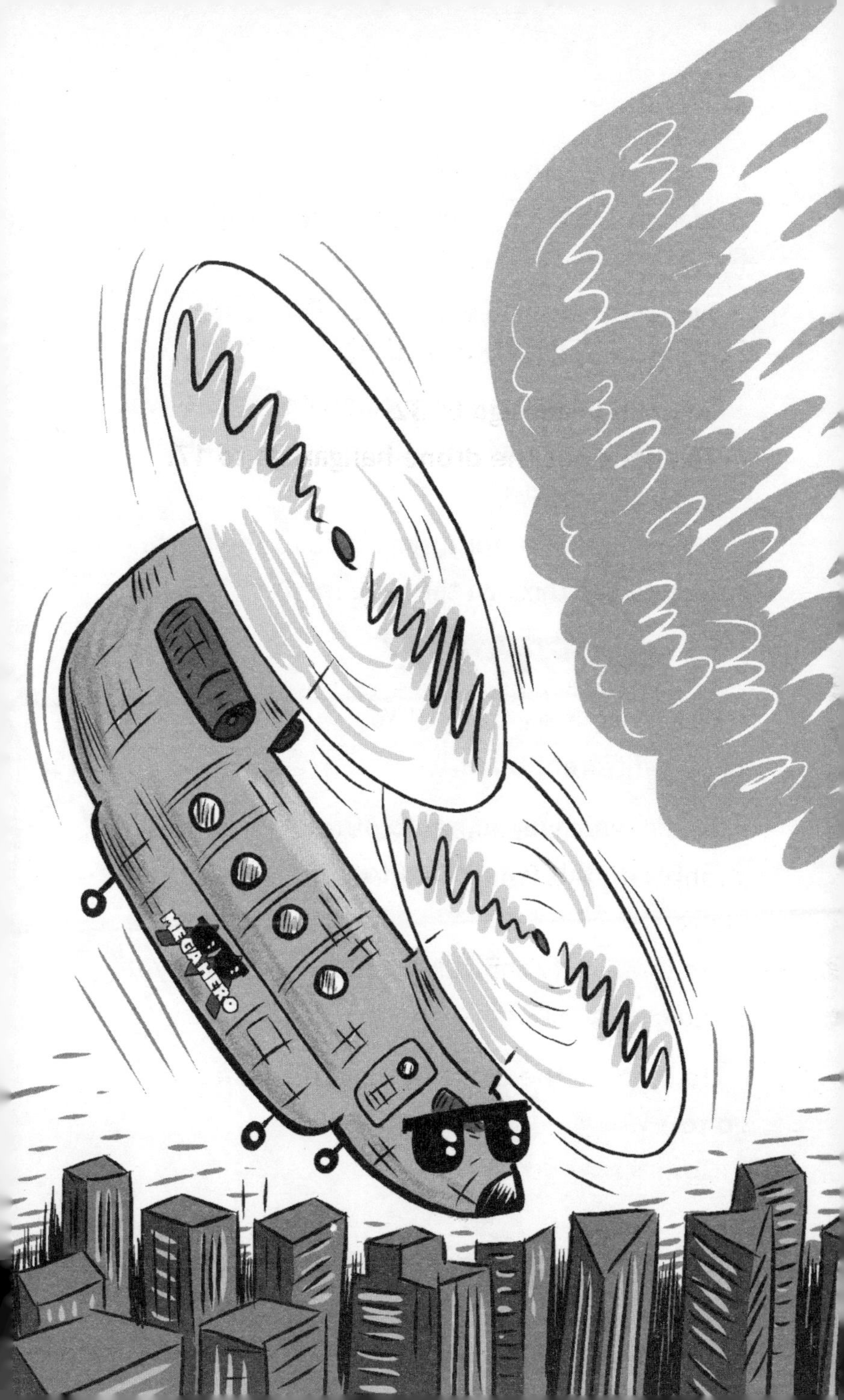
MEGA HERO

24

"I need to sneak in. Turn me into a mouse," you tell PAL.

Suddenly, you find yourself unable to move and start clicking.

"How will I sneak in as a computer mouse, you crazy computer? I meant a four-legged one!"

"SORRY," says PAL.

In animal mouse form, you race to the fence and try to get through the wire mesh.

ZAAPPPPPPPPO!

The fence is electrified! You're going to have to try a different plan!

To dig your way in, go to 30.

To blast your way in, go to 4.

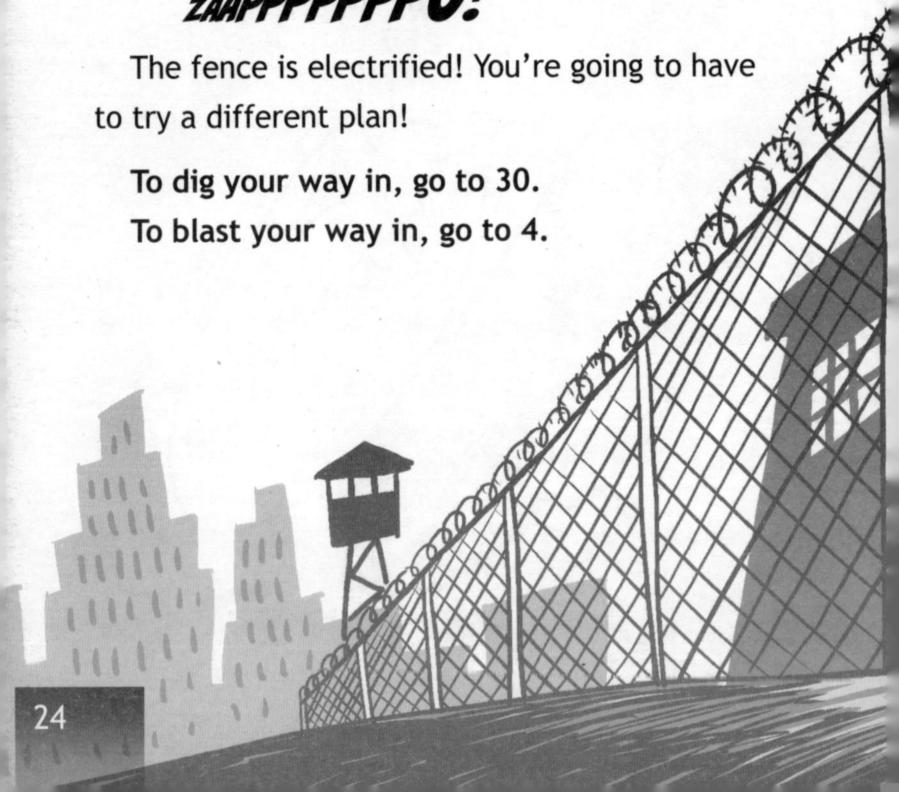

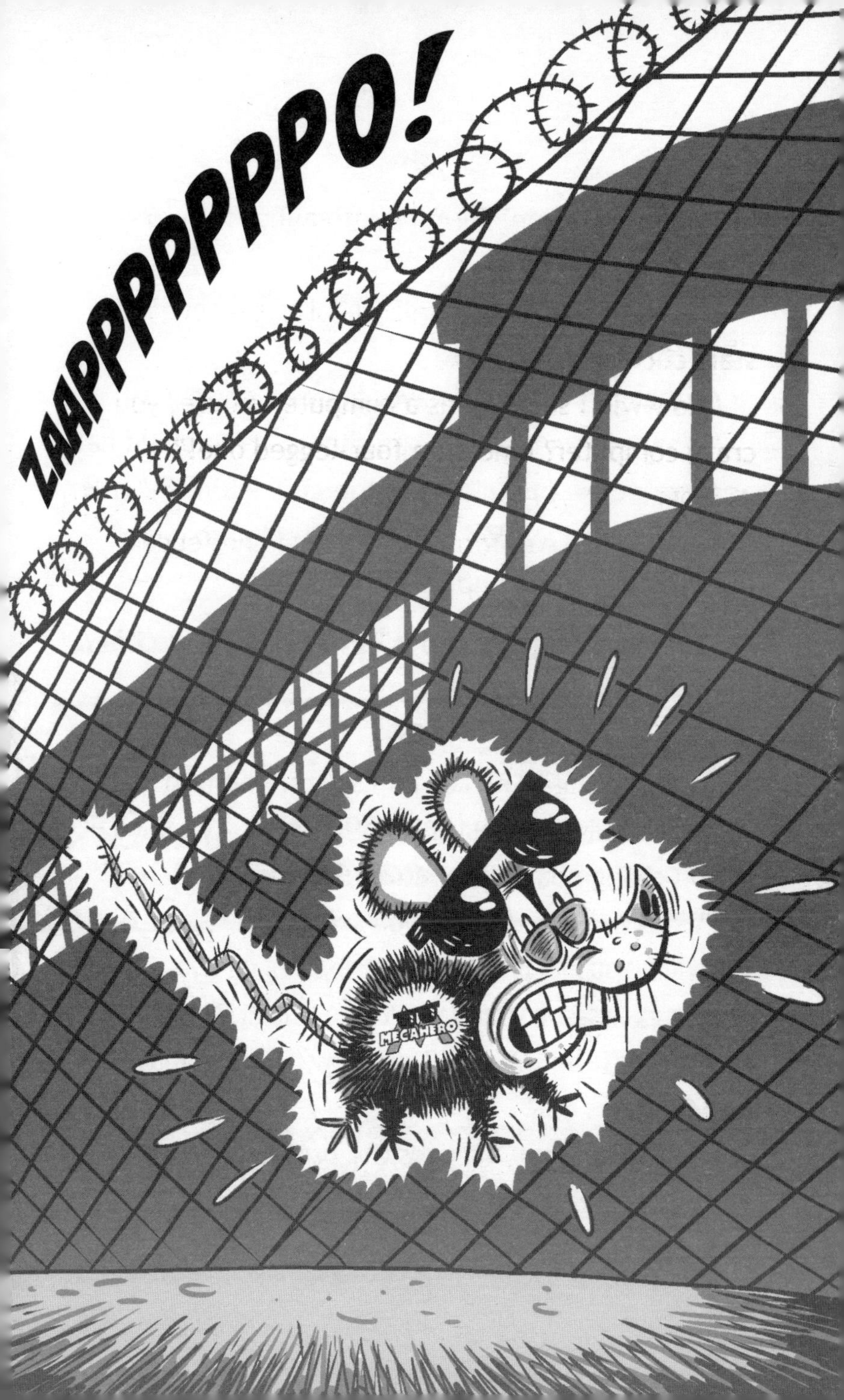
ZAAPPPPPPPO!
MECAHERO

25

"We need to know who we are dealing with," you say firmly. "I'll wait."

The search does take some time. "I DID WARN YOU ..." says PAL.

At that moment the mayor appears on screen.

"What are you doing?" she shouts. "The cloud has penetrated every building in the city — **EVERYONE** is hairy. You're a *MEGA* failure! I'm going to get a **PROPER** hero to help. You're fired!"

The mayor's got you out of her hair! *Go back to 1.*

26

"PAL, I'm going to attack him so turn me into something big and nasty!"

You change back into *MEGAHERO* form.

"What are you doing?" you scream.

"WELL, YOU ARE BIG AND YOU'RE BEING NASTY TO ATTACK **PROFESSOR WEIRD** WHEN HE'S SURRENDERED!"

"But he'll be **LYING**!" you say. "That's what *MEGA* villains do!"

"You're so right," laughs the professor. "I've got lots of gas left!"

Go to 15.

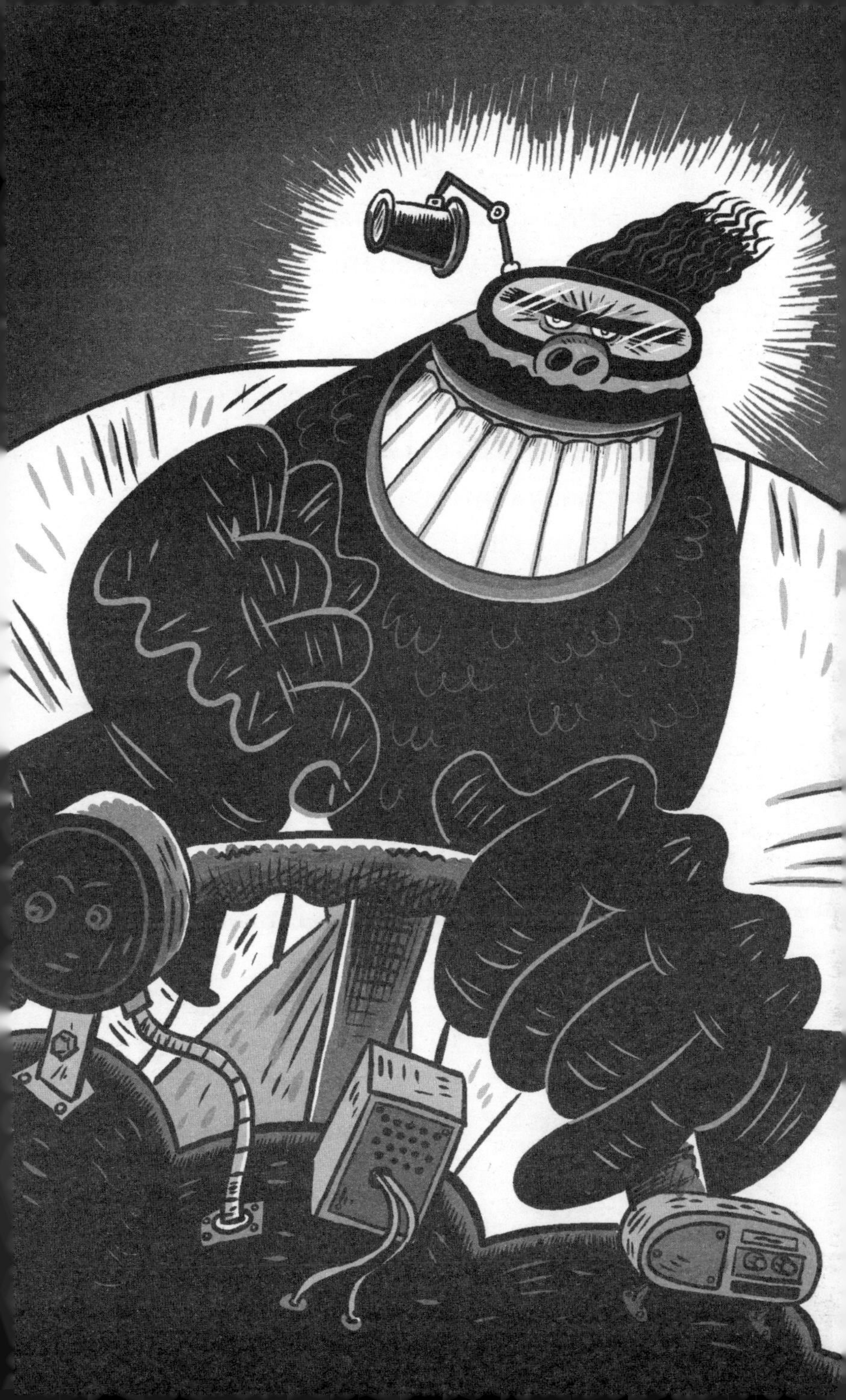

27

"There's no time to lose! I'm heading out to search for the prof," you tell PAL. "Turn me into a tracker dog."

"THAT IS A **BAD DECISION**!" says PAL.

"You have an attitude problem, PAL. I'm the ***MEGAHERO*** so please do as I ask!"

PAL reluctantly turns you into a dog and you head out into the city. However, despite hours of searching, there's no sign of Professor Weird.

Go to 3.

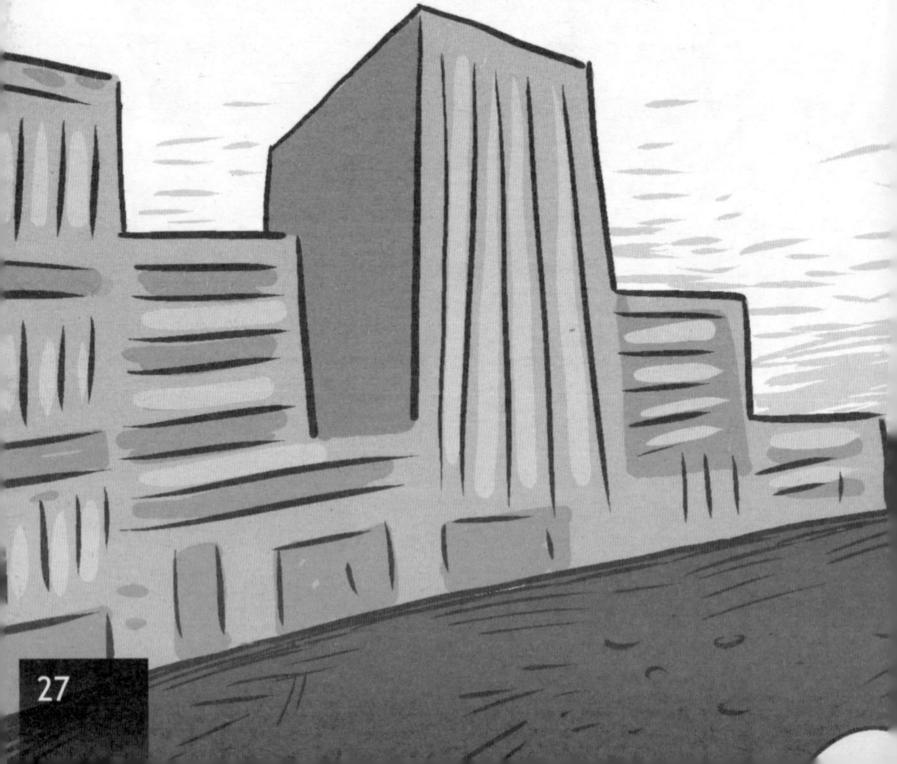

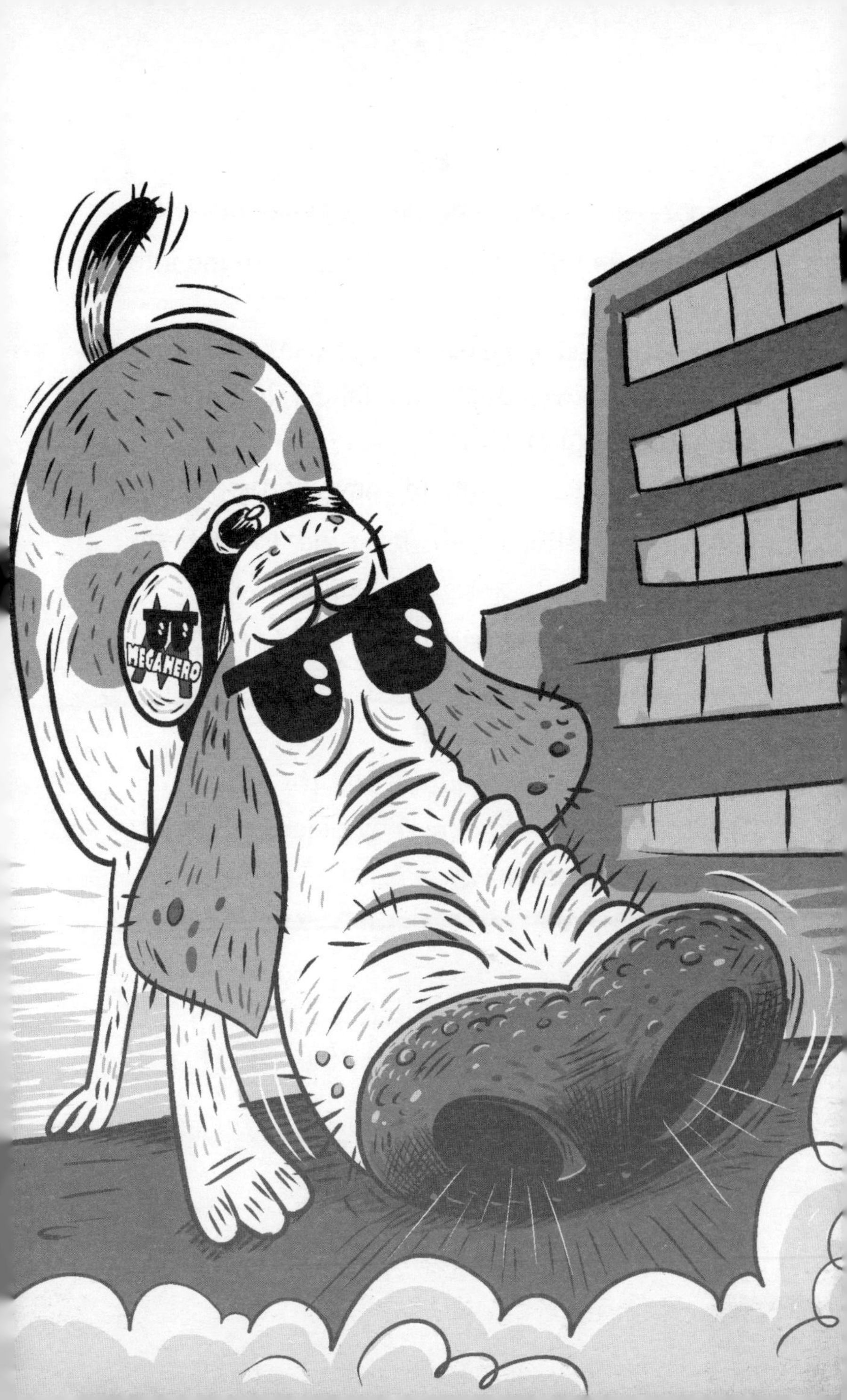
MEGAHERO

28

"Turn me into something that can take out the drones," you tell PAL.

The computer turns you into a taxi!

"YOU CAN TAKE THEM OUT IN THAT," says PAL.

"I meant '**TAKE OUT**' as in **DESTROY** them, not **TRANSPORT** them!"

PAL's mistake is fatal. You have no time to stop the drones as they fly off ready to unleash doom on the city!

You've failed! *Go back to 1.*

29

"Turn me into a parachute!" you cry.

PAL turns you into two shiny-black high heels and you plummet down.

"I said, a **PARACHUTE**, not a **PAIR OF SHOES**!" you cry.

PAL obeys and you float safely down to the ground. You look up to see that the cloud has disappeared from view.

“You have got to sort your hearing out,” you tell PAL.

“RUBBISH **IN**, RUBBISH **OUT**,” replies PAL moodily.

If you asked PAL to run a check on suspects, go to 16.

If you didn’t, go to 3.

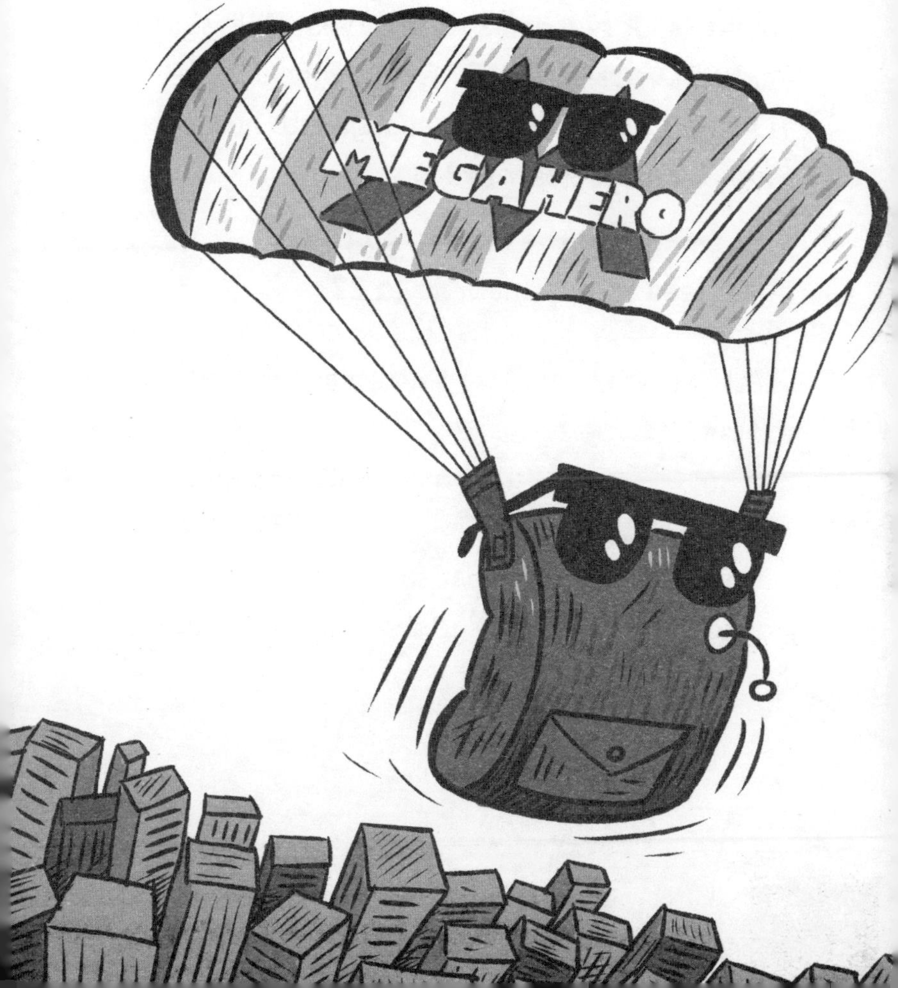
MEGAHERO

30

"Turn me into a digger."

Suddenly, you are very small and can hardly see. "A mole! Nice one, PAL!"

You start to burrow beneath the fence at ***MEGA*** speed. PAL guides you under the ground and into the chemical factory. You tunnel out and spot two doors head of you. One is marked **DRONE HANGAR**, the other, **TOP SECRET LAB**. You change into human form to take a closer look.

To head into the hangar, go to 17.

To head into the lab, go to 22.

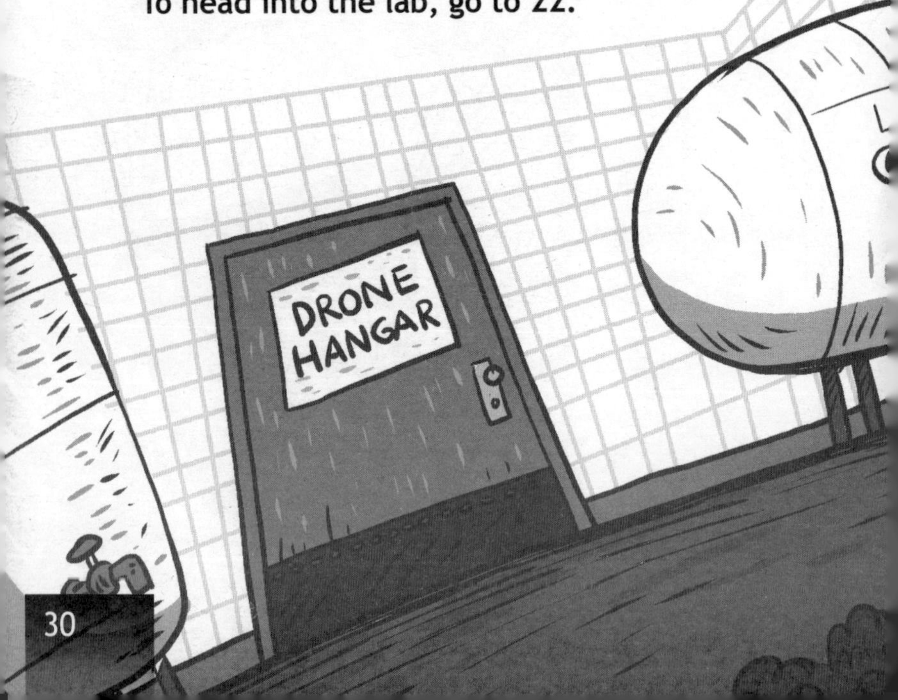
DRONE
HANGAR

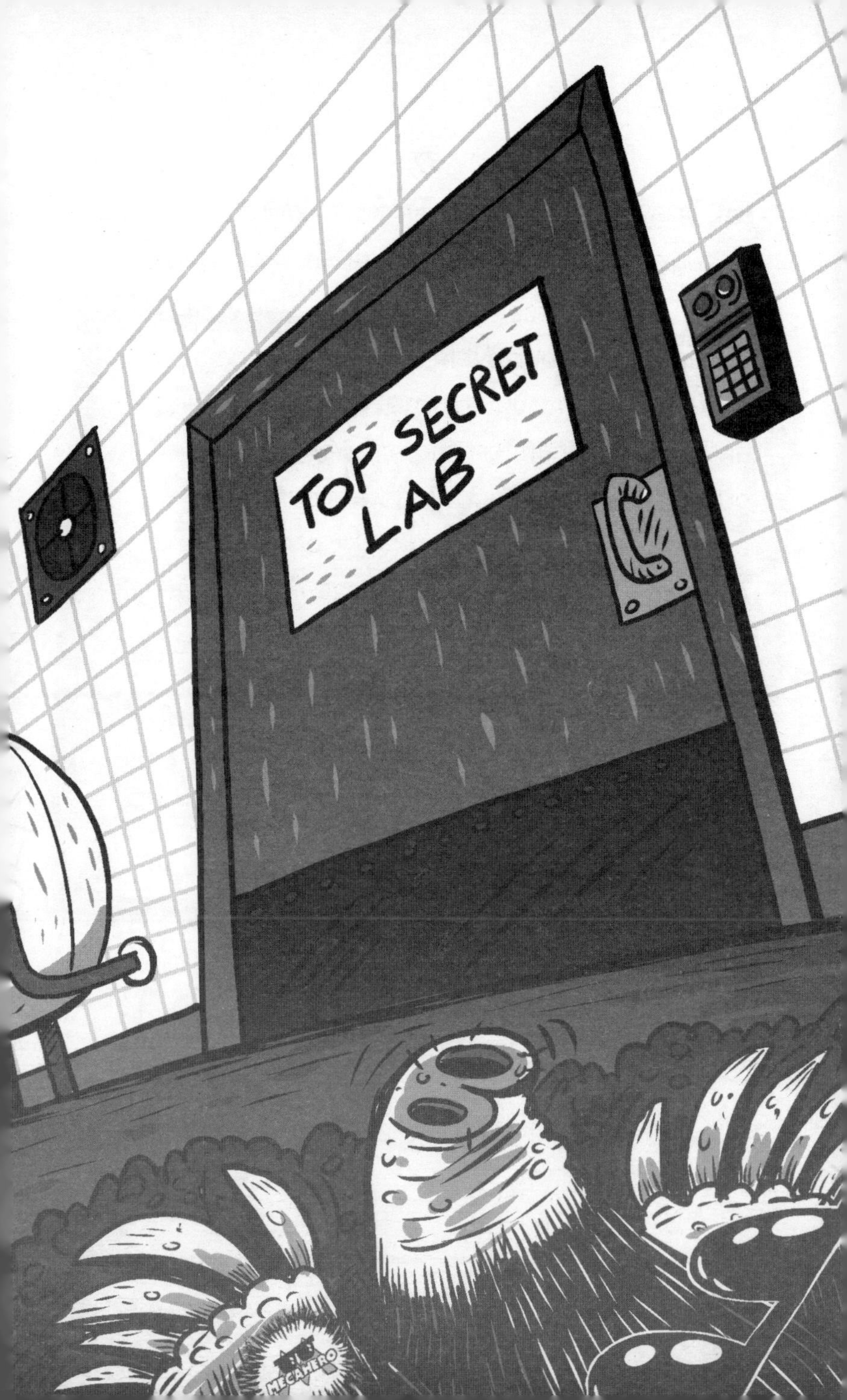
TOP SECRET
LAB
MEGAHERO

31

PAL brings up the file on Professor Weird.

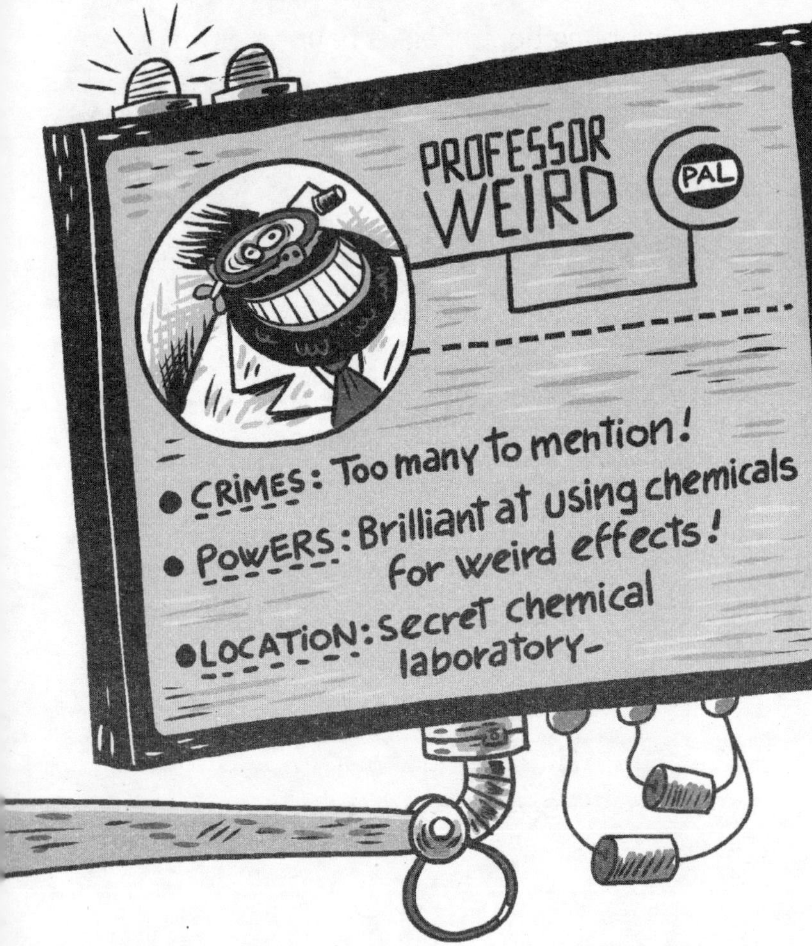
PROFESSOR WEIRD
PAL
• CRIMES: Too many to mention!
• POWERS: Brilliant at using chemicals for weird effects!
• LOCATION: secret chemical laboratory-

Go to 10.

32

You head inside and gasp. The room is bare!
The door slams shut behind you.

Green bubbling liquid begins pouring out of a
wall vent. You try to contact PAL but there is no
signal. The deadly chemical begins filling
the room ...

DA-DA-DAAAH!

How weird, you fell for the trap!
Go back to 1.

33

"With all respect, ma'am, I think you need a
hairdresser not a **MEGAHERO**."

"You don't understand," trembles the mayor.
"The whole city has a hair problem and only you
can fix it!"

The mayor's hair continues to grow and you
realise she really does need your **MEGA** help.

Go to 18.

34

The professor sends a cloud of gas your way, but you are ready for it!

"Okay, PAL, let's reverse the flow!"

PAL turns you into a ***MEGA HAIRDRYER***!

"***MEGA*** power!" you order. The dryer blasts the cloud of gas and blows it back towards the professor!

"***NOOOOOO!***" he cries as the cloud engulfs him. Hair begins to sprout, turning him into a ***MEGA*** hair ball. The flying car drops to the floor under the weight.

Once the cloud has dispersed, you turn back into human form.

"I hate you, Megahero!" cries the hairy ball lying on the floor.

"Stop moaning and keep your hair on!" you laugh.

Go to 50.

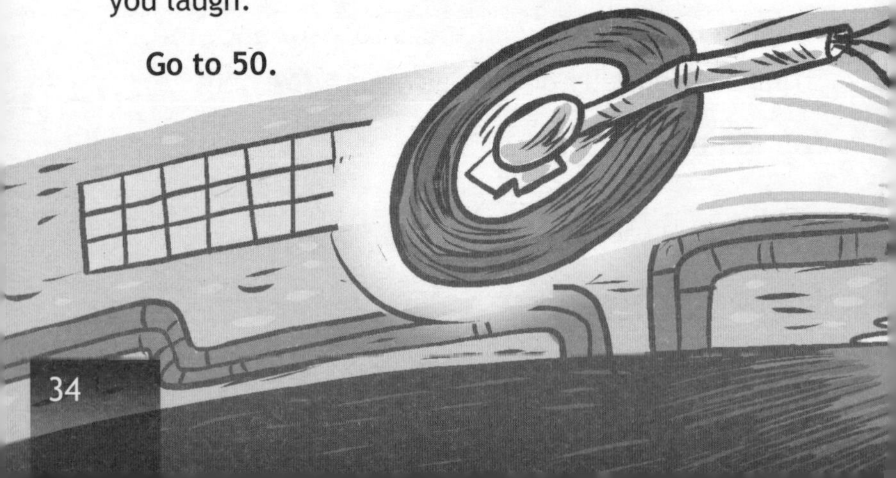

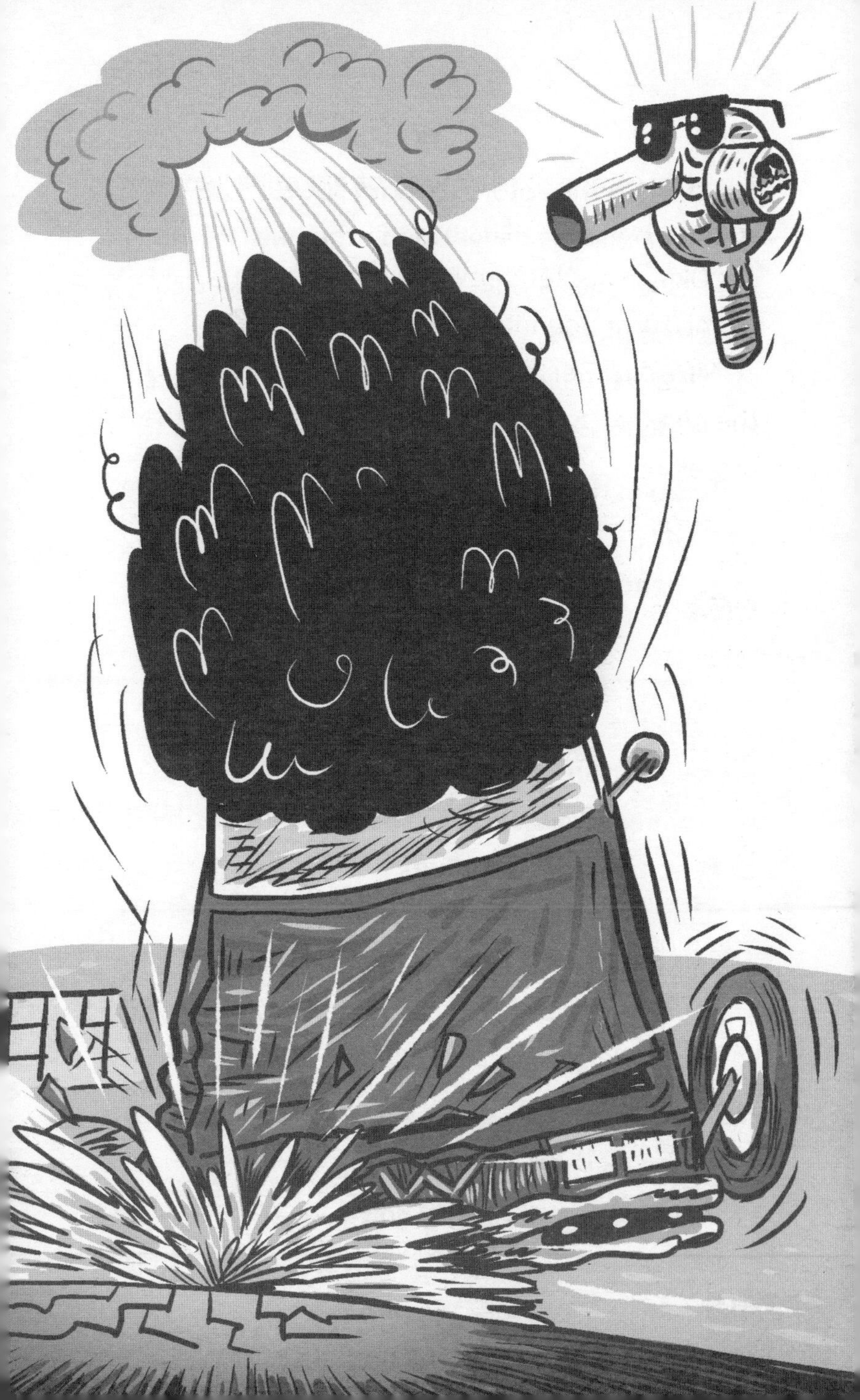

35

You turn up the rotors to **MEGA** speed. The cloud machine is caught up in the blast of air. It smashes into a building and explodes into a thousand pieces.

"THAT WAS OUR ONLY LEAD!" says PAL. "HOW ARE YOU GOING TO FIND **PROFESSOR WEIRD** NOW?"

To investigate the wreckage of the machine, go to 41.

To head back to the *MEGA* cave, go to 3.

36

You tail the cloud. You are amazed as it takes evasive action, zigzagging through the city skyscrapers. You increase speed but find it hard to keep up with the cloud.

"Any idea why this is happening?" you ask PAL.

"NO. I DON'T HAVE ENOUGH INFORMATION. I COULD TURN YOU INTO A FALCON," says PAL. "YOU COULD FLY INTO THE CLOUD, ANALYSE IT AND SEE HOW IT IS BEING CONTROLLED."

To agree to PAL's suggestion, go to 5.

To remain as a drone, go to 11.

"Why are you doing this hair and bald stuff?" you ask. "It's just weird!"

"The clue is in my name. It's weird because I am. It shows that I can control the extremes! It's hair today, then gone tomorrow! And if the mayor doesn't want her citizens to be hairy or bald then she is going to have to pay me lots of money! MWAHAHAHAHAHA!"

"Why does every **MEGA** villain laugh like that?" you ask, playing for time.

"It's part of the job description," the professor replies.

To attack the professor, go to 15.

To hide, go to 12.

38

"THE CLOUD IS THE ONLY LEAD WE'VE GOT SO DON'T LOSE IT LIKE YOU DID LAST TIME!" PAL says.

PAL turns you into a supersonic rocket and you shoot off. In the blink of an eye, you locate the pink cloud engulfing the streets. Looking down and using your ***MEGA*** vision you can see it turning people bald!

To fly into the cloud, go to 20.
To destroy the cloud, go to 23.

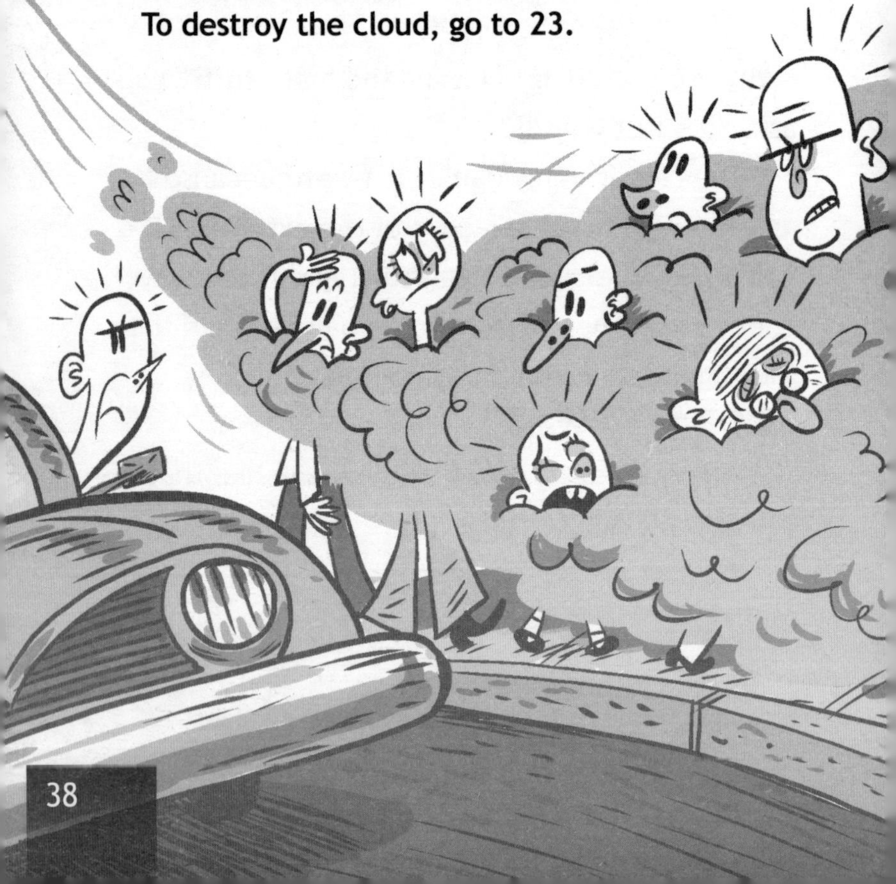

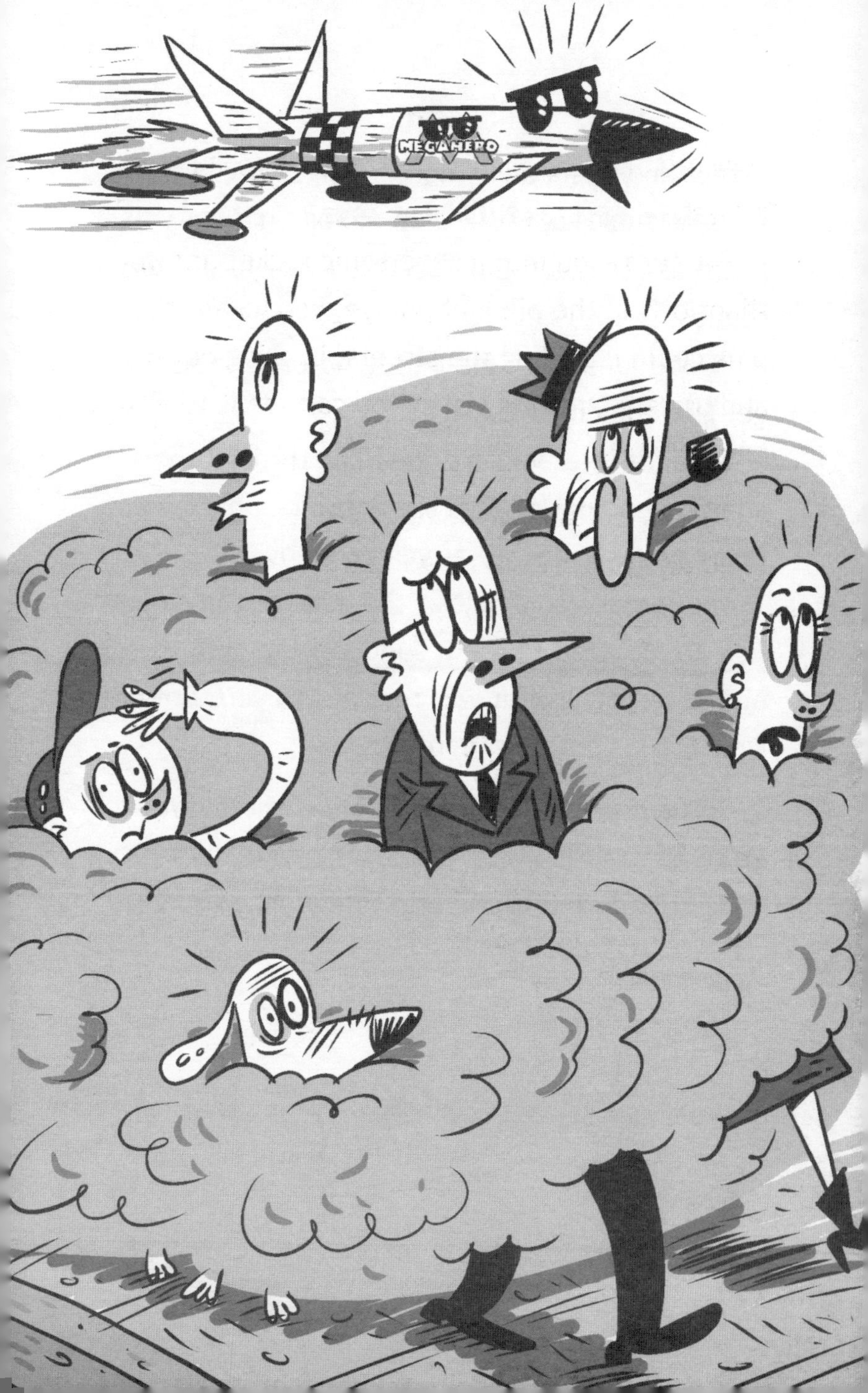
MEGAHERO

"What do you mean by non-organic?" you ask PAL.

"SOMETHING LIKE A MACHINE, SO YOU CAN'T BREATHE IN ANY OF THE CLOUD AND TURN INTO A HAIR BALL!" **PAL** replies.

"Good idea. Turn me into a motorcycle so I can get into the city **ASAP**!"

Seconds later you are speeding through the streets heading towards the green cloud. Hairy people stop and stare as you zoom by.

You screech to a halt at the edge of the cloud and are amazed to see it suddenly rise into the air and speed off as if it was reacting to your arrival! *How is that possible?* you wonder.

To turn into a falcon and follow the cloud, go to 5.

To turn into a drone and follow it, go to 21.

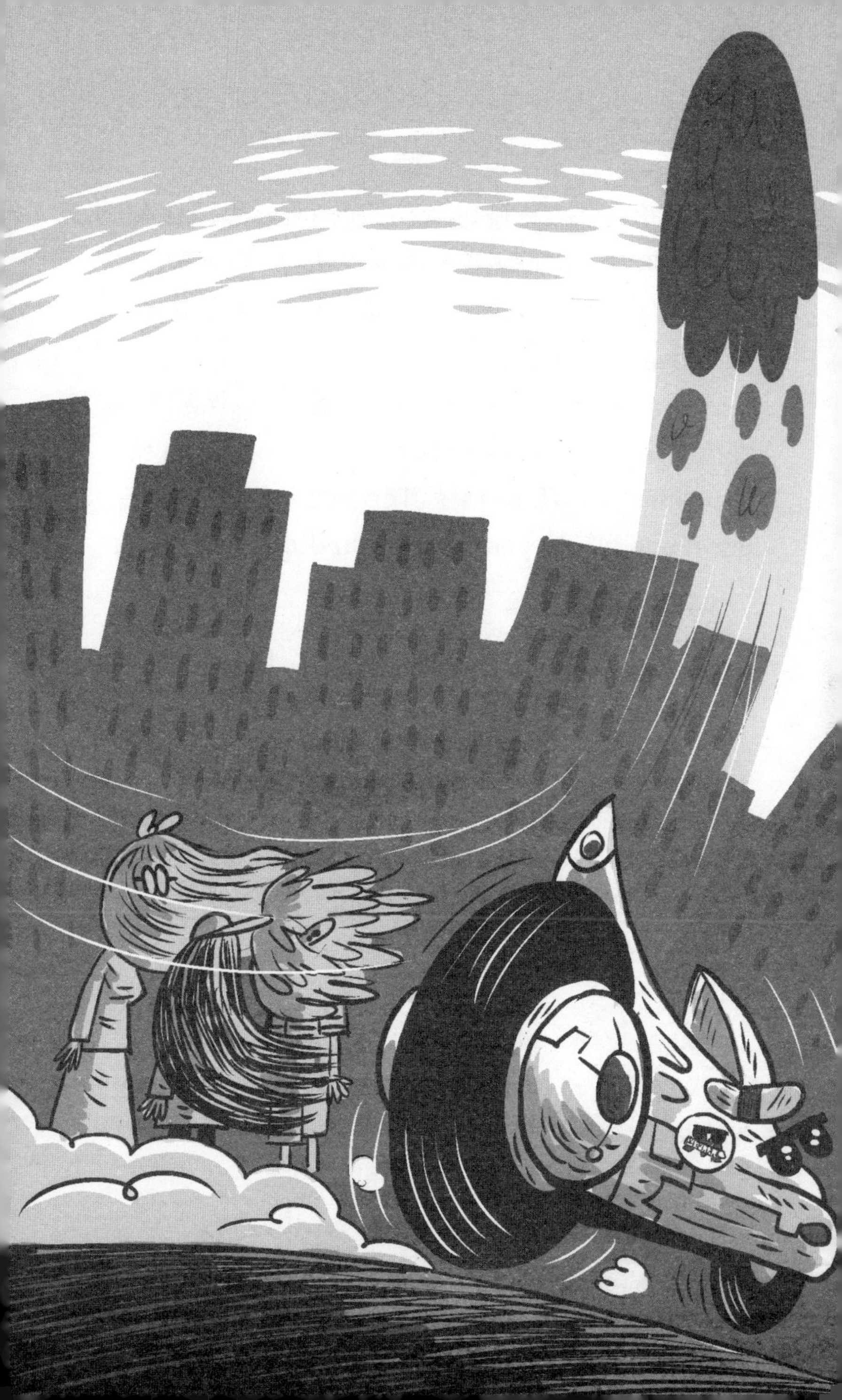

40

"You can't change because you've just breathed in my **ANTI-CHANGE CHEMICAL!**" laughs the professor. "Prepare to meet your weird end! Goodbye, **MEGAHERO**!"

A stream of purple liquid shoots from the flying car, covering you from head to toe. You begin to grow hair at a **MEGA** rate. The hair weighs you down and blocks your lungs. You drop to the floor.

DA-DA-DAAAH!

You're having a bad hair day! **Go back to 1.**

41

You fly down to the ground and turn back into **MEGAHERO** human form.

You pick through the mangled wreckage of the machine and find the damaged navigation control unit.

You plug the unit into your **COMMS** system.

"Where was this being controlled from?" you ask PAL.

"COORDINATES 345-987-623," it replies.

"Turn me into a jet car and set the coordinates."

PAL obeys and you zoom off. Minutes later you find yourself outside a huge chemical factory.

Go to 13.

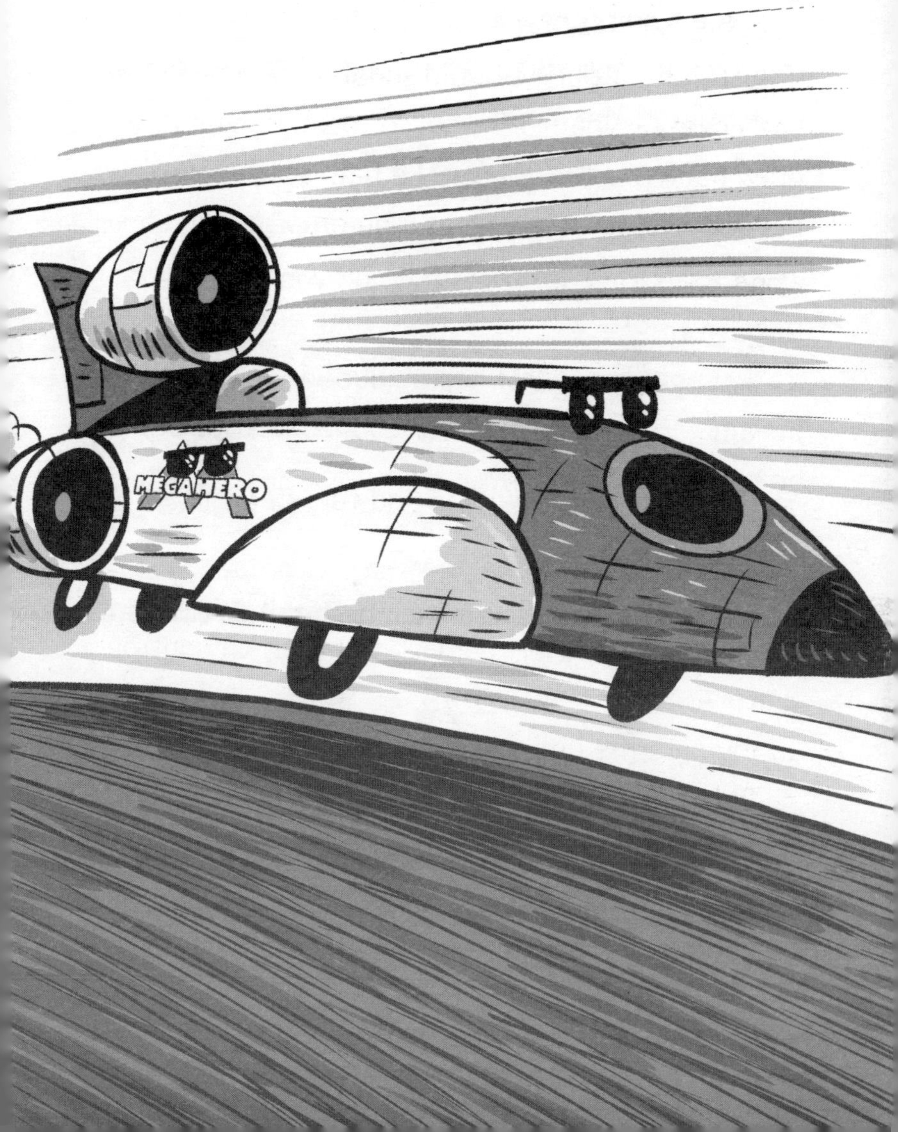
MEGAHERO

You head into the heart of the green cloud.

"Switch on chemical analysis systems," you order PAL.

There's no reply. You realise that the cloud is too thick for signals to get through. You spin around to get out of the cloud.

BANG!

OOPS! *Who put that building there?* you wonder. Your rotor blades fail and you plummet through the air.

"PAL, get me out of here!" But your cries are in vain — there's no time for communications to be restored!

DA-DA-DAAAH!

You're heading for a smashing time! *Go back to 1.*

Go back to 1.

43

"We need to close the roof and stop them getting out."

PAL turns you into a spider! Using **MEGA** speed, you **ZOOM** up the wall and spin a web across the roof opening.

The drones press against the ***MEGA*** web but can't break through. They crush against each other, causing their electrical circuits to overheat and spark.

KABOOM!

The drones splinter into millions of pieces.

You turn back into human form.

Now to find Professor Weird, you think.

Go to 2.

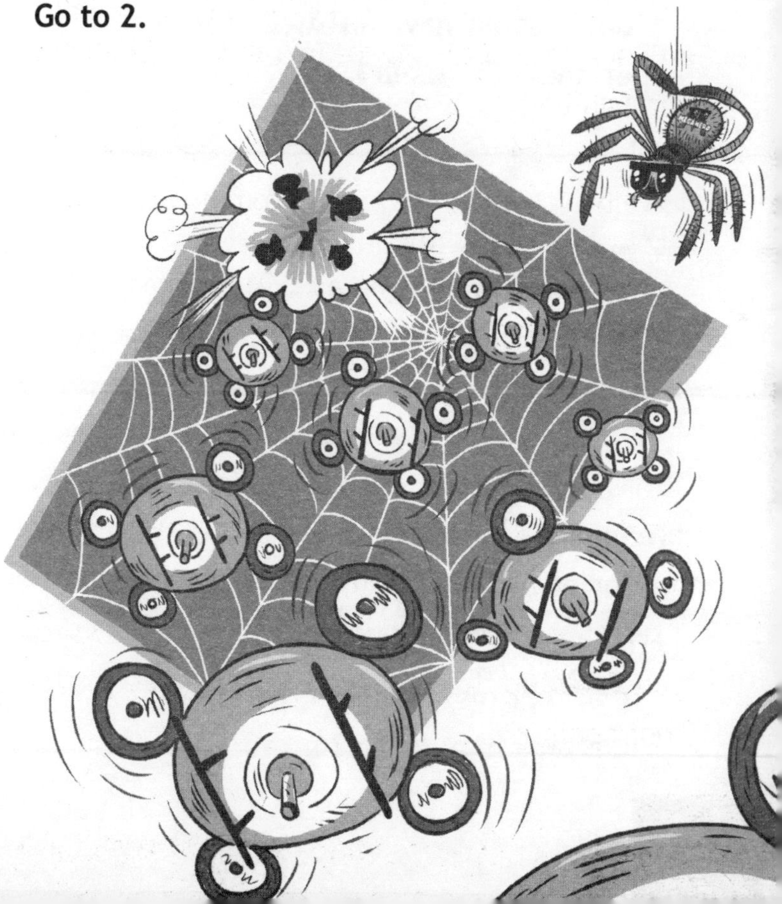

44

"Turn me into a helicopter, QUICKLY!" you order.

PAL obeys, but you've made a *MEGA BAD* mistake! The electrical circuits are still fried and your rotors are not turning! You continue to fall through the sky with no time to change into something else!

DA-DA-DAAAH!

You're about have a HARD learning experience! *Go back to 1.*

45

"PAL, I can't breathe in that gas!"

You instantly become a *MEGA* gas mask!

"That's *MEGA* brilliant, PAL! Sometimes you get it *soooo* right!"

Professor Weird shoots another cloud at you, but it has no effect! He tries again and again. But you are immune to his attack.

Finally, he stops. "All right, Megahero, you win. I surrender. I've run out of gas!"

To accept his surrender, go to 6.
To attack him, go to 26.

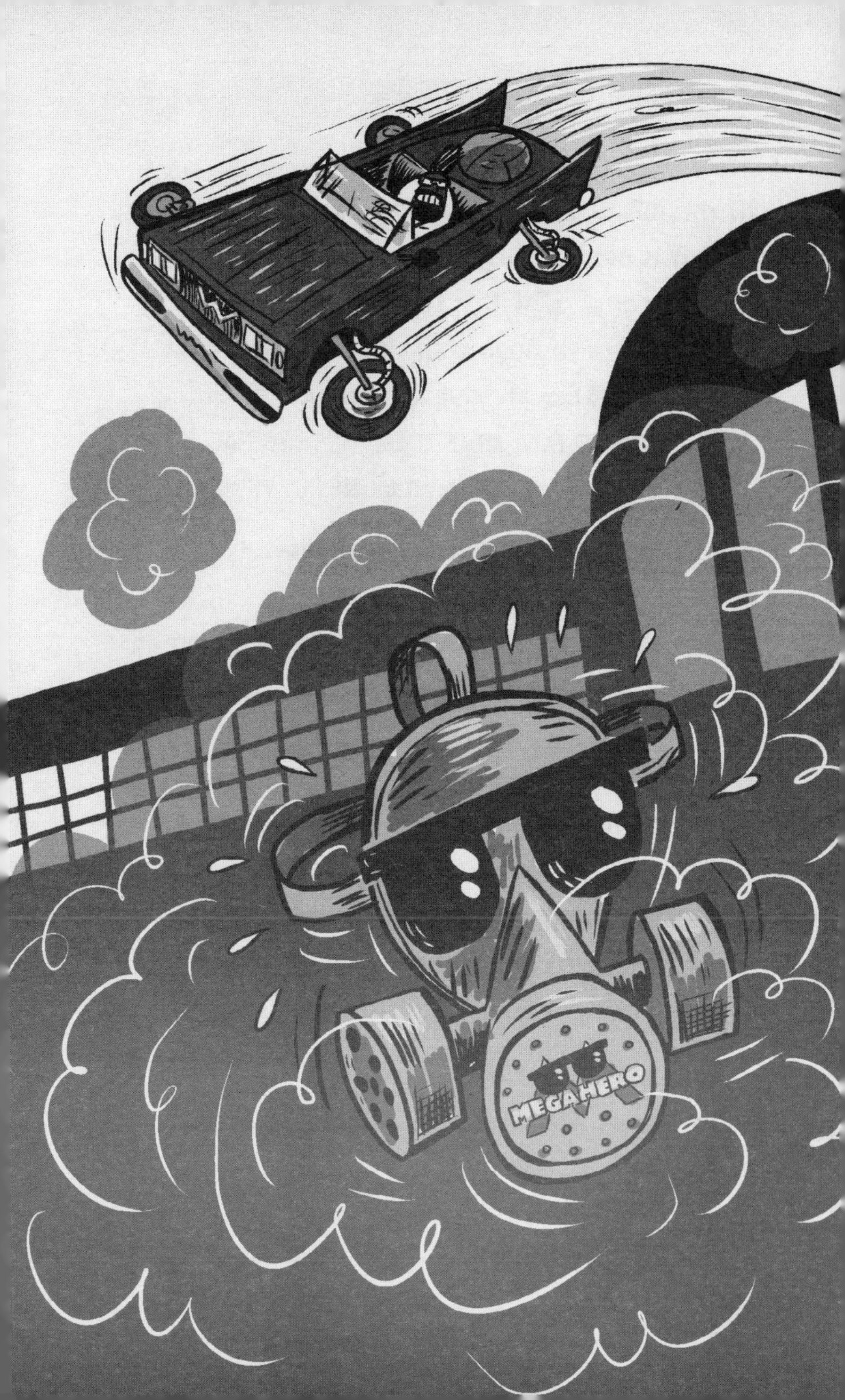
MEGAHERO

46

"If the mayor is right and some *DASTARDLY MEGA VILLAIN* is behind this," you tell PAL, "then we need to come up with a list of possible suspects. Run the facts through your database and see what **BADDIES** are out and about."

"THAT COULD TAKE SOME TIME," replies PAL. "THERE ARE SO MANY **MEGA VILLAINS** OUT THERE ..."

To investigate the cloud immediately, go to 8.

To wait for PAL to finish the check, go to 25.

47

"I'm going to find him **NOW** and find out why he's suddenly gone into the hair business!" you tell PAL.

"DON'T YOU THINK IT WOULD BE BETTER TO FIND OUT MORE INFORMATION ABOUT **PROFESSOR WEIRD**?" suggests PAL. "IT COULD SAVE YOU TIME LATER ..."

To get information, go to 31.

To get on with the mission immediately, go to 27.

48

You track the cloud-making machine for some time. Finally, the signal remains static before disappearing.

Hmmm, it's been switched off, you think. You fly to the machine's final position and find yourself outside a huge chemical factory.

Go to 13.

49

PAL turns you into a peregrine falcon and you speed off.

Reaching the city, you see the green cloud hanging over the streets. Below you, people and animals stagger about weighed down by their hair!

As you arrive the cloud seems to sense your presence and begins to move away at speed!

Go to 5.

50

You drop the professor off at the local jail and head back to the **MEGA** cave, where the mayor is waiting to talk to you via video link.

"The effects of the gas have worn off and everyone's hair seems to be growing back to normal," she says.

"So, the professor's hair-brained schemes didn't pay off this time!" you reply.

The mayor nods. "Thanks to you, the city escaped by a hair's breadth!"

You smile. "No problem, ma'am. It's all part of the job of being a **MEGAHERO**!"

The End!

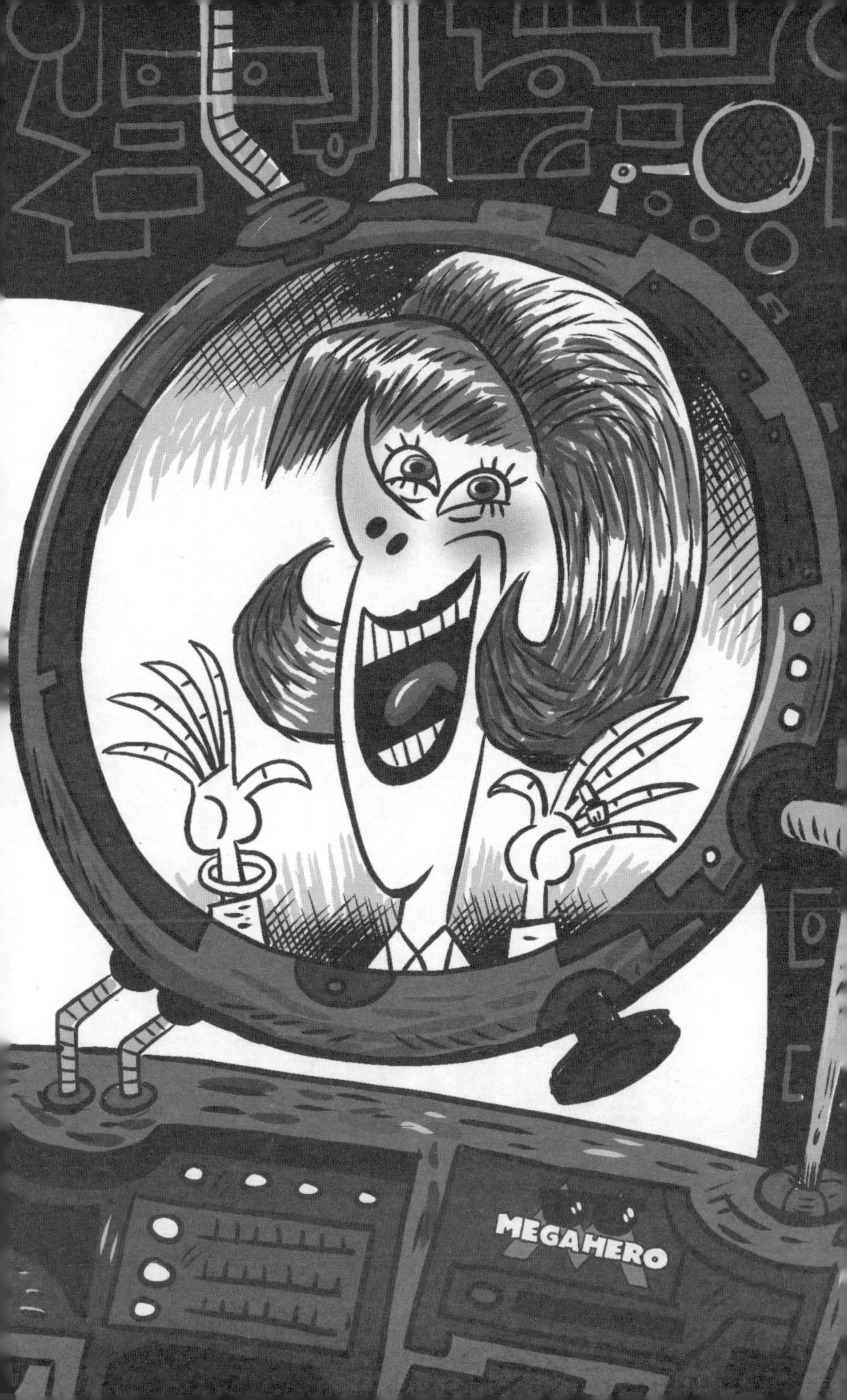
MEGAHERO

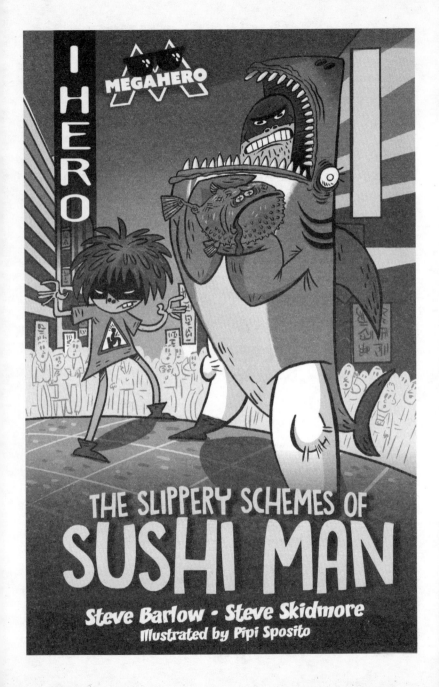

THE SLIPPERY SCHEMES OF
SUSHI MAN

Steve Barlow · Steve Skidmore
Illustrated by Pipi Sposito

You are at your holiday home in the Bahamas, swimming with dolphins — which is even more fun when you can turn into a dolphin yourself!

The earphones in your **MEGASHADES** start beeping, and the **Augmented Reality** screens in the lenses flash.

Your **MEGACOMPUTER**, PAL, has an urgent message.

"I'M GETTING REPORTS OF A CRIME WAVE IN JAPAN."

"No problemo," you say. "I'm always ready to kick supervillain butt."

"THE ROBBERS AREN'T SUPERVILLAINS," says PAL. "THEY'RE ORDINARY PEOPLE. OFFICE WORKERS AND SHOP ASSISTANTS ARE ROBBING BANKS AND HOLDING UP SECURITY VANS."

"That is strange," you say. "Time to use my **MEGAMORPH** powers!"

To fly to Japan in bird form, go to 12.
To turn into a jet fighter, go to 28.

CONTINUE THE ADVENTURE IN:

THE SLIPPERY SCHEMES OF
SUSHI MAN

About the 2Steves

"The 2Steves" are
Britain's most popular
writing double act for
young people, specialising
in comedy and adventure.
They perform regularly in
schools and libraries, and at festivals, taking the
power of words and story to audiences of all ages.

Together they have written many books, including the
I HERO Immortals and *iHorror series*.

About the illustrator:
Pipi Sposito

Pipi was born in Buenos Aires in
the fabulous 60's and has always
drawn. As a little child, he used
to make modelling clay figures, too.
At the age of 19 he found out
he could earn a living by drawing. He now develops
cartoons and children's illustrations in different
artistic styles, and also 3D figures, puppets and
caricatures. Pipi always listens to music when he works.

Have you completed these I HERO adventures?

I HERO Immortals – more to enjoy!

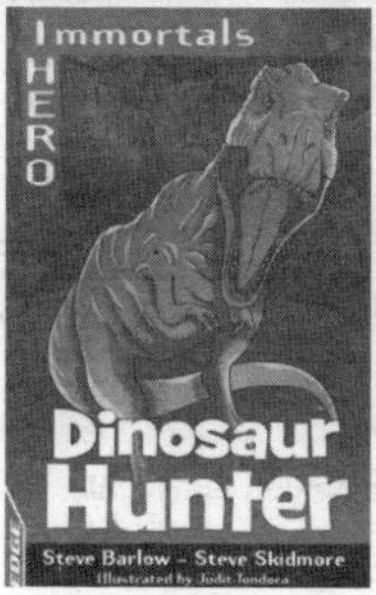
Immortals
HERO
Dinosaur Hunter
Steve Barlow – Steve Skidmore
Illustrated by Judit Tondora

978 1 4451 6963 7 pb
978 1 4451 6964 4 ebook

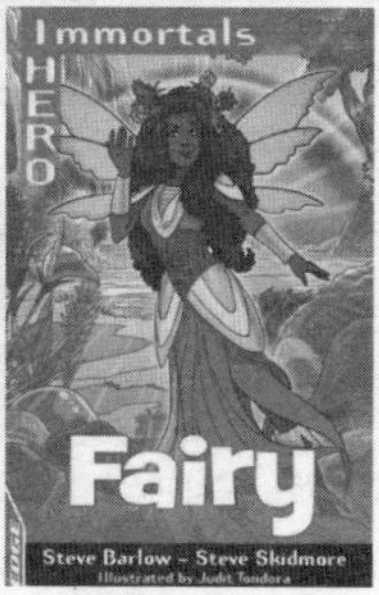
Immortals
HERO
Fairy
Steve Barlow – Steve Skidmore
Illustrated by Judit Tondora

978 1 4451 6969 9 pb
978 1 4451 6971 2 ebook

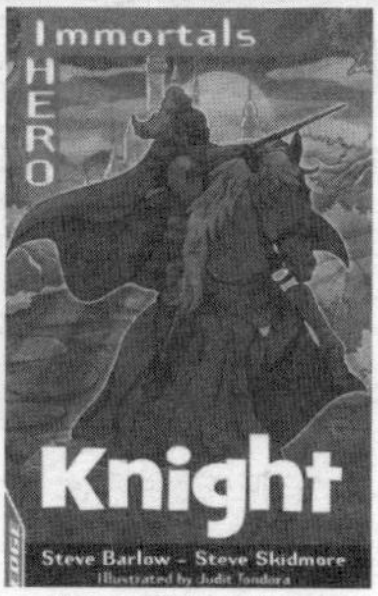
Immortals
HERO
Knight
Steve Barlow – Steve Skidmore
Illustrated by Judit Tondora

978 1 4451 6957 6 pb
978 1 4451 6959 0 ebook

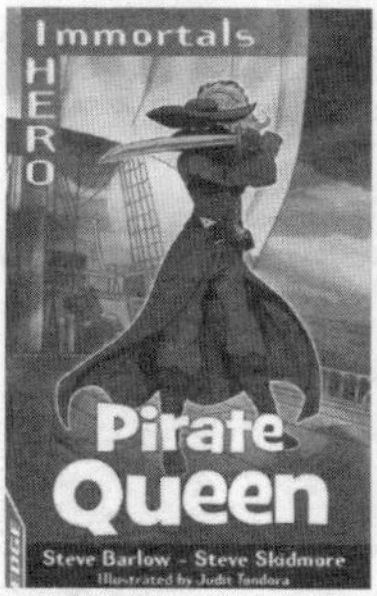
Immortals
HERO
Pirate Queen
Steve Barlow – Steve Skidmore
Illustrated by Judit Tondora

978 1 4451 6954 5 pb
978 1 4451 6955 2 ebook

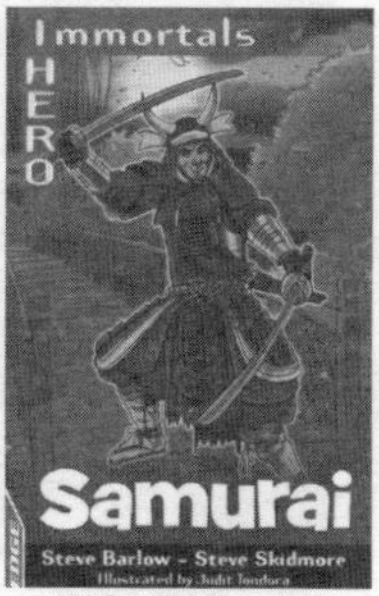
Immortals
HERO
Samurai
Steve Barlow – Steve Skidmore
Illustrated by Judit Tondora

978 1 4451 6960 6 pb
978 1 4451 6962 0 ebook

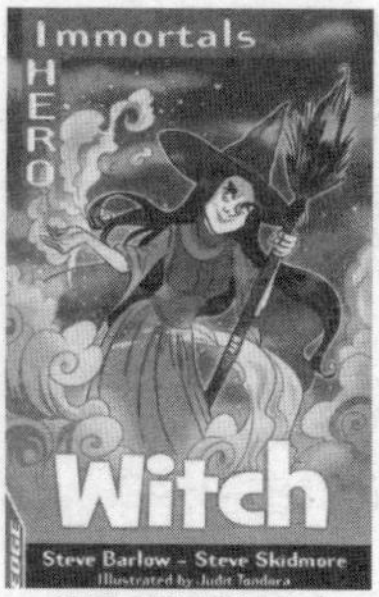
Immortals
HERO
Witch
Steve Barlow – Steve Skidmore
Illustrated by Judit Tondora

978 1 4451 6966 8 pb
978 1 4451 6967 5 ebook

Defeat all the baddies in Toons:

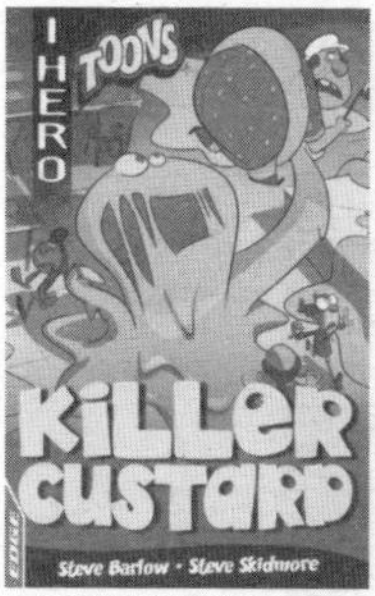
I HERO
TOONS
KiLLeR CUSTaRD
Steve Barlow • Steve Skidmore

978 1 4451 5930 0 pb
978 1 4451 5931 7 ebook

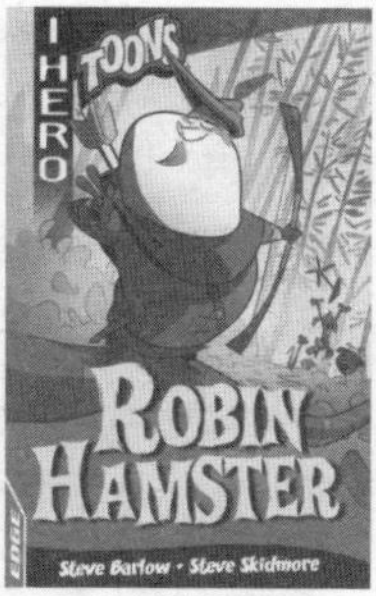
I HERO
TOONS
ROBIN HAMSTER
Steve Barlow • Steve Skidmore

978 1 4451 5921 8 pb
978 1 4451 5922 5 ebook

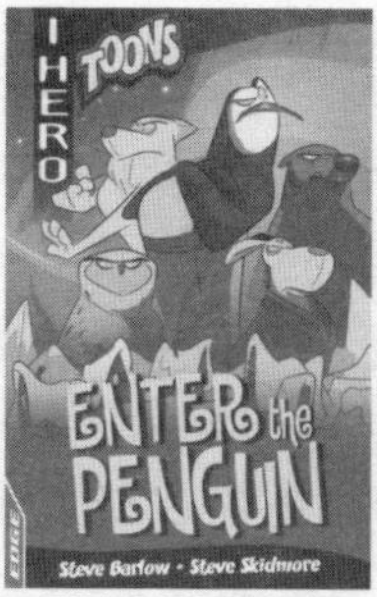
I HERO
TOONS
ENTER the PENGUIN
Steve Barlow • Steve Skidmore

978 1 4451 5924 9 pb
978 1 4451 5925 6 ebook

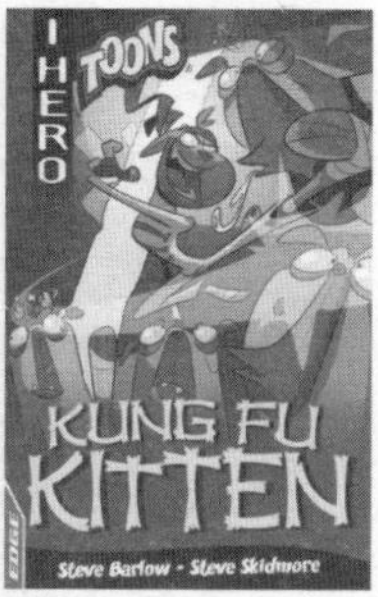
I HERO
TOONS
KUNG FU KITTEN
Steve Barlow • Steve Skidmore

978 1 4451 5918 8 pb
978 1 4451 5919 5 ebook

Also by the 2Steves...

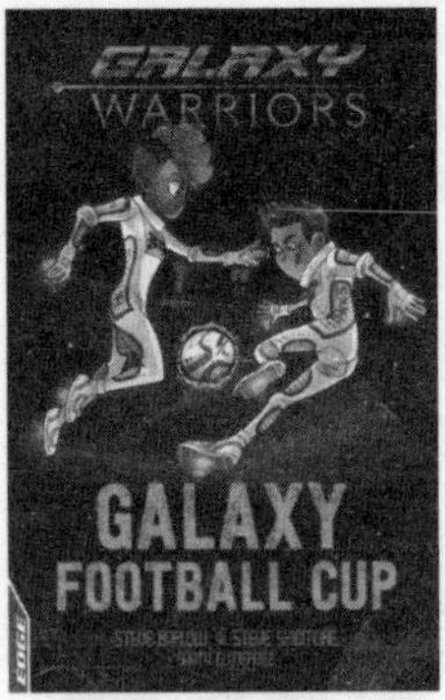
GALAXY
WARRIORS
GALAXY
FOOTBALL CUP

978 1 4451 5985 0 hb
978 1 4451 5986 7 pb

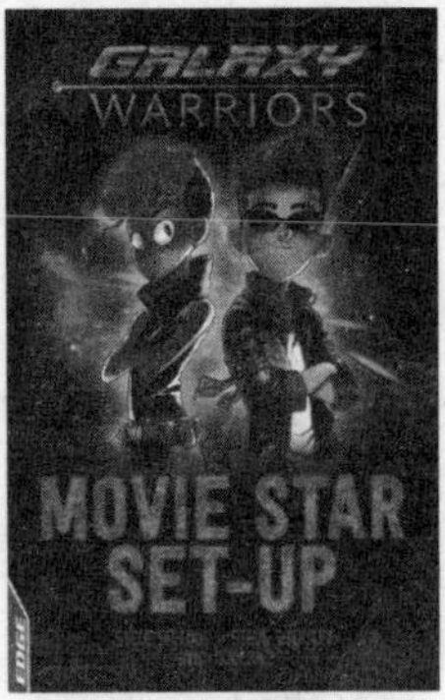
GALAXY
WARRIORS
MOVIE STAR
SET-UP

978 1 4451 5976 8 hb
978 14451 5977 5 pb

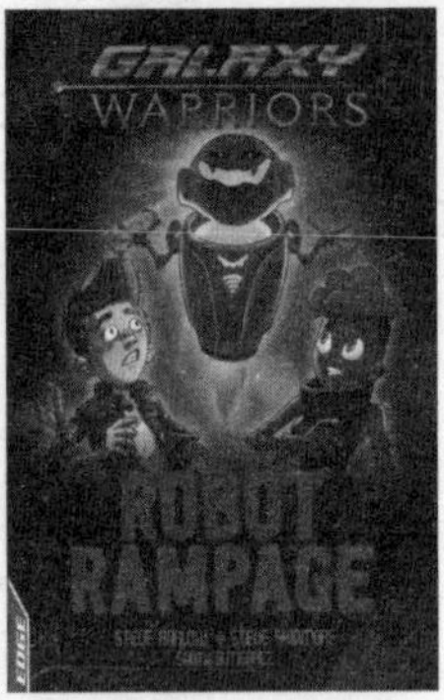
GALAXY
WARRIORS
ROBOT
RAMPAGE

978 1 4451 5982 9 hb
978 1 4451 5983 6 pb

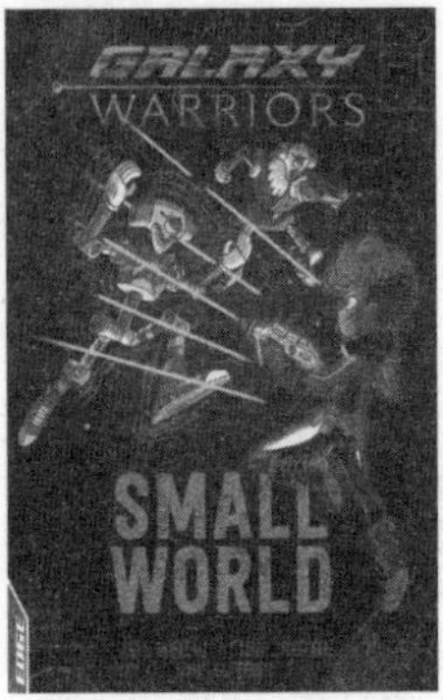
GALAXY
WARRIORS
SMALL
WORLD

978 1 4451 5972 0 hb
978 1 4451 5971 3 pb

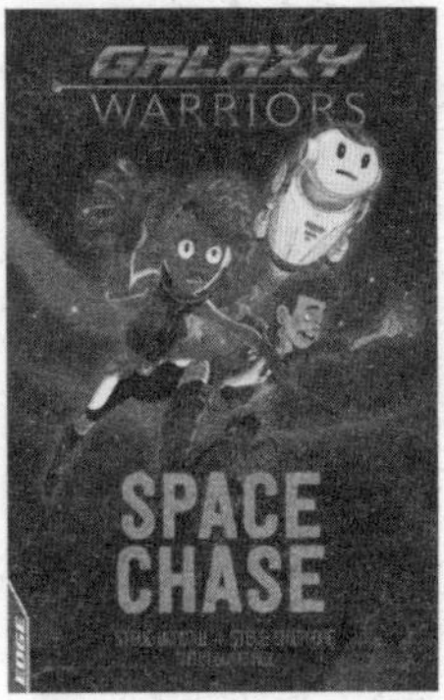
GALAXY
WARRIORS
SPACE
CHASE

978 1 4451 5892 1 hb
978 1 4451 5891 4 pb

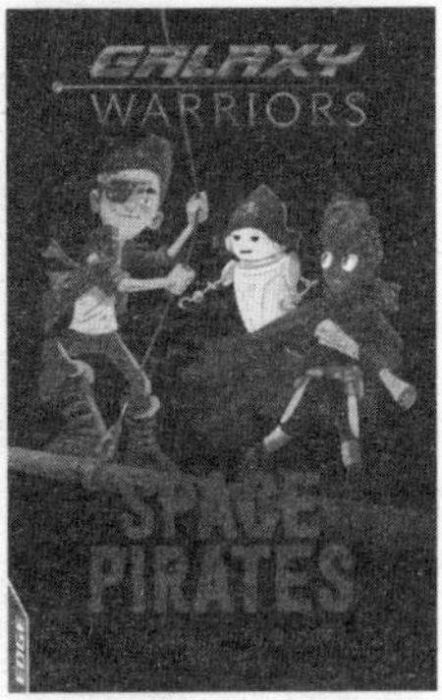
GALAXY
WARRIORS
SPACE
PIRATES

978 1 4451 5988 1 hb
9781 4451 5989 8 pb

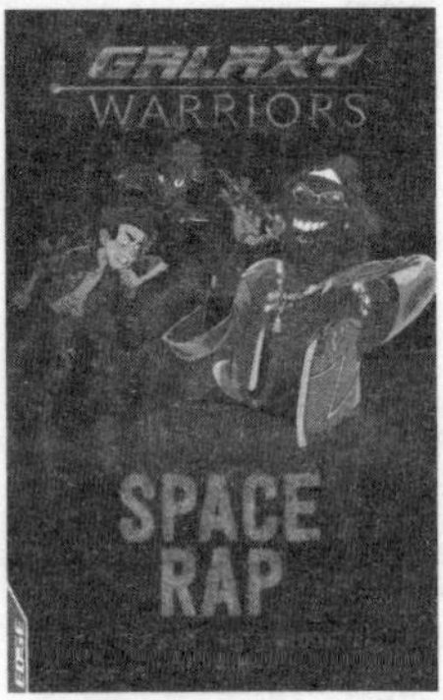
GALAXY
WARRIORS
SPACE
RAP

978 1 4451 5973 7 hb
978 1 4451 5974 4 pb

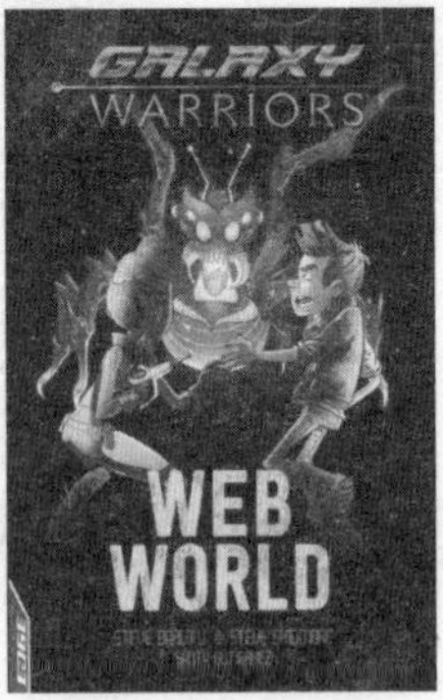
GALAXY
WARRIORS
WEB
WORLD

978 1 4451 5979 9 hb
978 1 4451 5980 5 pb